"Too bad you couldn't change your name," Tanner said, half-joking.

"Then your ex would be looking for Laura Jessup and not Laura someone else." Suddenly, a crazy, ridiculous, ludicrous idea flitted through his brain. "How open are you to harebrained schemes?"

She lifted her head, gave a soft chuckle. "Why? Do you have one?"

Something twisted in his gut, in an oh-my-God-are-you-really-going-to-ask way. His palms started to sweat and his breath caught. He'd said the words once before in his life, but this time it was different. This time it wasn't for love. So why was he so tied up in knots?

"I just might. And you're going to be tempted to say no, but hear me out."

Her brows pulled together in a puzzled look.

"Laura," he said, not quite believing what he was about to say. "I think we should get married."

Dear Reader,

In 2006, I sold my first book to Harlequin. It featured a heroine who was pregnant and a hero who came to the rescue by offering a solution to her troubles in the form of marriage. He also loved her child as his own. *Hired by the Cowboy* is still a fan favorite.

Fast forward to 2016, and my twenty-ninth book for Harlequin, and I've done it again. If you read *The Cowboy's Christmas Family*, you'll know a bit about Laura Jessup and her newborn baby girl, and you'll have met Tanner Hudson, the rancher and EMT who helped deliver her baby.

The baby is not his, but he loves her just the same. He offers Laura a way out of her problems by proposing a marriage of convenience—for just as long as it's convenient. The thing that's not convenient? Attraction. Friendship. Love.

Love, marriage, a baby in a carriage? I love writing stories where that order is all mixed up. It's hard on my characters, but the resulting happy-ever-afters are some of my favorites.

I hope they're yours, too.

Happy reading,

Donna

THE COWBOY'S CONVENIENT BRIDE

———

DONNA ALWARD

HARLEQUIN® AMERICAN ROMANCE®

Recycling programs
for this product may
not exist in your area.

ISBN-13: 978-0-373-75601-8

The Cowboy's Convenient Bride

Copyright © 2016 by Donna Alward

Printed in U.S.A.

Donna Alward is a busy wife and mother of three (two daughters and the family dog), and she believes hers is the best job in the world: a combination of stay-at-home mom and romance novelist. An avid reader since childhood, Donna has always made up her own stories. She completed her arts degree in English literature in 1994, but it wasn't until 2001 that she penned her first full-length novel and found herself hooked on writing romance. In 2006, she sold her first manuscript, and now writes warm, emotional stories for Harlequin.

In her new home office in Nova Scotia, Donna loves being back on the east coast of Canada after nearly twelve years in Alberta, where her career began, writing about cowboys and the West. Donna's debut romance, *Hired by the Cowboy*, was awarded a Booksellers' Best Award in 2008 for Best Traditional Romance.

With the Atlantic Ocean only minutes from her doorstep, Donna has found a fresh take on life and promises even more great romances in the near future!

Donna loves to hear from readers. You can contact her through her website, donnaalward.com, or follow @DonnaAlward on Twitter.

Books by Donna Alward

Harlequin American Romance

The Cowboy's Christmas Family

Crooked Valley Ranch

The Cowboy's Christmas Gift
The Cowboy's Valentine
The Cowboy's Homecoming

Visit the Author Profile page
at Harlequin.com for more titles.

To Johanna and all the editors at Harlequin who have come before...I've learned so much from you and have enjoyed every minute. #editorappreciationsociety

Chapter One

Tanner Hudson was getting sick of the bar scene.

Unfortunately, the other option was to hanging out at home, which was nearly as bad. Particularly when his older brother, Cole, and his girlfriend, Maddy, always sat around making googly eyes at each other.

Tanner lifted his glass and took a sip of his Coke, listening to an old George Jones song on the jukebox. He scanned the room for a friendly face. The last thing he wanted this evening was a woman. His lips curved in a wry smile. He was sure that no one would believe that for a second. He knew his reputation. Cole was the steady, reliable one. Tanner was the younger brother who worked hard and played hard and liked the ladies. He set down the Coke and scowled at it. On the surface, people were right. But deep down, well, that was another story. He was pretty darn good at keeping up appearances.

Rylan Duggan walked into the Silver Dollar, dusting a few flakes of spring snow off his hat. Tanner perked up. Rylan was a friendly face, and they had a lot in common. When Ry scanned the room, Tanner lifted his chin in a quick greeting, and Rylan grinned.

Tanner got up and met his friend at the bar. Rylan

ordered a beer, and as he was waiting, Tanner put a hand on his shoulder. "Hey, buddy. Am I glad to see you."

Rylan chuckled. "Why? You want to try to win back the money you lost last time?"

When they happened to be in the same place at the same time, Tanner and Rylan would often shoot a game or two of pool. Last time, Tanner had lost a twenty.

"Sounds fine to me. Slow in here tonight."

Rylan took his beer and looked at Tanner, as if trying to puzzle him out. "Kailey's off to some potluck supper and candle party or jewelry or...well, I wasn't really paying attention. I thought I'd drop by for a burger. What brings you here? The Dollar isn't usually your speed."

Tanner shrugged, the dissatisfaction nagging at him again. "Bored, I guess. Hell, Ry, I live in a house with my parents and big brother." He shook his head. "I should get my own place or something." His own life, perhaps.

"Why don't you?"

They made their way over to the pool tables. Tanner was kind of embarrassed to answer the question, actually. It came down to two things: money and convenience. The convenience thing was understandable, so he went with that. "I'm working the place with Cole and Dad. It just makes sense to, you know, be close."

Rylan nodded. "I get it. And it can get claustrophobic, too." He started setting up the balls. "I lived in my RV until Kailey and I moved into Quinn's old place. The last thing I wanted was to be under the same roof with Quinn and Lacey, especially when they were newlyweds."

Tanner selected a stick and chalked the end. "Tell me about it. I love Maddy, I really do, but she and Cole are all in love and everything, and they're around a lot."

"I get it, bro." Rylan removed the triangle and reached for a stick, testing the feel of it in his hand. "Maybe you should settle down. Could be that's your problem. Restless feet."

Tanner laughed. "Right." Rylan's statement hit a little too close to home, though. Truth was, Tanner was pretty sure there was more to life than this.

He lined up and broke, balls scattering over the table.

"Naw, I'm telling you," Rylan said. "Married life is pretty good. I never wanted to settle down, either, until Kailey. Now I know what I was missin'." He grinned, a little sideways smile that made Tanner roll his eyes.

Tanner missed his next shot, so it was Ry's turn. As Tanner watched, he let out a dissatisfied sigh. Everywhere around him, people were in love and telling him how wonderful it was. And it wasn't that Tanner wasn't happy for his brother. He was. Maddy was a great woman, with adorable kids, and he was pretty sure wedding bells would be ringing for his brother really soon.

Tanner just wasn't sure he was built that way. Or that he was the marrying kind. He was, as his ex put it, *built for fun, but not for a lifetime*.

Fun he could do. Because he sure as hell wasn't interested in having his heart stomped on again. So he worked hard and blew off some steam now and again. As far as the living-at-home thing, he'd been young and stupid and had spent his money as fast as he'd made it. But not in the last few years. He'd saved what he would have paid on rent or a mortgage until he'd built up a nice little savings. His truck wasn't new, and other than what little he spent on going out, his expenses were few.

Maybe he wasn't a keeper in the love department, but no one would ever accuse him of being broke and worthless again. Maybe he should bite the bullet and put a down payment on a place of his own.

Trouble was, it wasn't just living at home that was making him itch. It was the ranch, too, and feeling as if his whole life was laid out in front of him. No deviation. No curve balls. It was so…predictable. He didn't hate the ranch; it wasn't that at all. But he couldn't shake the feeling that there might be something more out there waiting for him.

"Dude. It's your shot. You off in la-la land or what?"

Tanner frowned. "Sorry. I'm probably not very good company tonight."

"No kidding. At this rate, you're going to be down another twenty."

Mad at himself for being bad company, Tanner let out a breath and focused on sinking the next ball. He did, and two more, which made him feel as if he was a little more with the program.

They finished the game and Rylan asked if he wanted to play another, but Tanner just wasn't in the zone. "Sorry, man," he said. "I'm out. But I'll take that twenty."

"Come on. Double or nothing. I'm here for another two hours until Kailey's done."

Tanner thought about it, but then he shook his head. "I'm bad company anyway. You should get yourself some suicide wings and a few more beers and find another willing victim."

Rylan laughed and dug in his wallet for the twenty. It seemed like each time they met, the bill just exchanged hands, back and forth. Tanner pocketed it and shrugged back into his denim jacket. "Thanks for the game, Ry."

"Anytime. And, Tanner? I wasn't kidding. Maybe you need to find yourself a woman. You know, to relieve all that pent-up tension." Rylan winked at him and Tanner laughed dutifully, but he was far too grouchy to be amused. Women were complicated creatures. They caused any number of troubles, had the ability to stomp on your heart and strip away your confidence. And yet they remained so damned desirable. They could make a man feel like a million dollars and as if he could conquer the world. Even if it was only for one night.

"I'll see you around, Ry. Thanks for the game."

More on edge than when he'd entered the Silver Dollar, Tanner crossed the parking lot to his truck and hopped in. He started the engine and turned on the wipers, letting them brush the light dusting of snow off the windshield. Flurries in April weren't that uncommon, though he was more than ready to leave winter behind for good. Longer days and warm temperatures should improve his mood, right?

He'd driven a little ways down the street when he spotted a car with its hood up in the bank parking lot. The bank was closed this time of night; whoever it was must have stopped to use the ATM, and it was the only car in the lot. As he slowed, he saw someone bent under the hood. By the shape of the snug jeans, it was a woman. And as much as Tanner considered women trouble, he wouldn't drive away from someone with car trouble. He put on his signal and pulled into the lot.

She stood up as he drove into the spot next to her, and he recognized her immediately. Laura Jessup. Well, if that didn't complicate matters… Laura had a new baby—and the rumor was that the father was none other than Maddy's late husband. He'd seen her a handful of times since Christmas. It had been a bit awkward, considering how the families were now connected. More for her than for him, really. He liked Laura. Admired her, too. Maybe she'd made mistakes, but she was handling them.

Tanner had been the volunteer EMT on duty the day she went into labor and called for an ambulance. He knew he wasn't supposed to let things get personal while on a call, but helping the single mom deliver her baby had been a different circumstance. It was a day he wouldn't ever forget.

"Laura, hi." He called out to her as he hopped out of the truck. "Having car trouble?"

She looked relieved to see him. "Hey, Tanner. I went into the bank and when I came out, my car wouldn't start."

"Let me try. I can always give you a boost."

"You're welcome to try and I appreciate it." She ran a hand over her hair, which was in a perky ponytail with little orangey-red strands sticking out. "My phone's out of juice and the baby's in the back. Sleeping, for now, thank God."

The baby. Tanner had ridden in the back of the ambulance on the way to the hospital and had been there for everything, including the final ten minutes in the emergency room when she'd delivered. He normally would have turned everything over to the doctors and nurses in the department, but Laura had grabbed his hand and asked him to stay. Begged him, so she wouldn't be alone.

He'd stayed. Right through to the moment the first cries echoed through the room and Laura had started crying herself. Then he'd stepped back and left the room, more affected than he should have been in his professional capacity.

That had been almost four months ago. As he passed by her to get to the driver's side of her car, he noticed that she definitely had her pre-pregnancy figure back. Well, maybe a few more curves, but they looked good on her. Real good. She looked more rested than she had the last time their paths had crossed, too. She must be adjusting to mom life. From what he heard, there wasn't a lot of sleeping going on for the first few months with a new baby.

Giving his head a shake, he slid behind the wheel and turned the key. There was a whirring noise, but it got slower and slower and nothing caught. He glanced into the back seat. The car seat was rear facing, so he couldn't see the baby's face—just the edges of a white frilly hat and a pink blanket.

As quietly as he could, he got out of the car. "Looks like we'll have to try giving you a boost," he said. "And looking at your car, I'd say you're probably due for a new battery."

"Damn it." Laura let out a big sigh. "Oh well. I

guess when you drive an older vehicle you have to expect some maintenance costs."

Tanner nodded. "I know. I go through the same thing with my truck. Hang on, I'll pull up closer and get my cables."

"Thanks, Tanner." She smiled at him. "Looks like you're coming to my rescue again."

His gaze met hers, and heat crept up his neck and into his face. He was blushing, for God's sake. And all because he'd covered for another paramedic that December day when her baby was born. It didn't get much more personal than that.

Well, that wasn't the only reason. Laura Jessup was extraordinarily beautiful. Tall, with a stunning figure, thick coppery hair, arresting blue eyes and a smile that went straight to a man's gut. The rumor was that Gavin Wallace had fathered her baby while he was still married to Maddy. Looking at Laura now, with her sweet smile and gratitude shining in her eyes, Tanner figured he could understand how Gavin had been attracted to her. Particularly since she and Gavin had been high school sweethearts. She'd be a hard woman to forget.

Of course, Maddy was now in love with Tanner's brother. Which made Tanner feel as if he was somehow betraying both Maddy and Cole just by thinking about Laura this way.

He jumped into the truck and maneuvered it so it was nearly bumper to bumper with hers, and then grabbed the cables from the back and hooked up the two batteries. "Okay," he said, "hop in and try it."

It whirred for a few moments, then sputtered and caught, roaring to life. Relieved, Tanner disconnected the cables and threw them in the back of the truck. Laura got out as he closed her hood.

"Tanner, thank you so much."

"It's no big deal. Glad the boost worked. You're probably going to need a new battery, though."

"I know."

"Do you have a charger at home? In case it doesn't start again?"

She shook her head. "No, but I'll get a new battery tomorrow. Promise."

He didn't argue. The garage would be closed now anyway. Unless she drove all the way into the city, there wasn't anywhere she could get a battery today anyway.

"I'll follow you home," he said. "In case it's not your battery, but your alternator or something. You'll know because you'll see your charge dropping."

"You don't have to…"

"If your phone's dead and you've got your daughter in the back…" He frowned. "I'd like to make sure you get home all right. It's just flurrying now, but what if it starts snowing harder?"

"In April?"

He snorted. "Come on, it wouldn't be a Montana spring without a few random storms."

"Fine," she replied. "And I appreciate it, Tanner. A lot." She hesitated, then met his gaze again. "Not everyone would stop and give me a hand."

It would have been less awkward had she not alluded to her persona non grata status in town. He'd often wondered why she stayed here, but figured it had to do with her grandparents. Or maybe it had been because of Gavin and now it was logistically too hard to move.

Still, she was a tough cookie for facing the community censure day in and day out. Whatever she had or hadn't done, she'd always been friendly and polite to him—before the baby and every time they'd run into each other since. Tanner tended to judge people on what he saw, rather than what he heard.

He smiled at her. "I'd never hear the end of it if I didn't help a neighbor in need," he said. "Besides, I'm sure you want to get the baby home."

"Her name's Rowan," she said quietly.

Rowan. There was something restful about the name that he liked. "That's pretty," he said, feeling inept at this sort of thing. How did a proclaimed bachelor make small talk about babies? He had a flash of inspiration. "She's healthy and everything?" Considering her fast entrance into the world, and that he was one of the EMTs that day, it seemed a logical question.

Laura smiled again as the car idled beside them. "Yes, perfectly. She likes to keep me up at night sometimes, but we just work around it."

"That's good," he replied. "And you look good, Laura. Rested. Whatever you're doing is working."

"Thanks." She smiled shyly. And then the silence became awkward again.

"Well, you head out and I'll follow you just in case."

"Sure thing. Thanks again, Tanner."

"Anytime."

She got in her car and he backed away, letting her out so she could lead. The snow was coming down a little harder now, and would be slick before the night was out if the temperature kept dropping. She lived in a little house just west of town limits, and when she turned into her driveway and gave a wave in her rearview mirror, he thought, as he had that day in December, how lonely it must be out here all by herself, with the neighbors spread out. Her name wasn't even on the mailbox.

Tanner turned around and headed back toward town and home. It wasn't until he passed the Silver Dollar again that he thought of Rylan and his comment that Tanner should go out looking for a woman.

If he did, the last one he should set his eyes on was Laura Jessup. She might be sweet as apple pie and gorgeous to boot, but she came with way more complication than he was interested in pursuing.

"LAURA, IS THAT YOU?"

Laura hadn't even shut the door when her grandfather called out to her. She closed her eyes and took a deep breath, then put Rowan's car seat on the floor. "Yes, Gramps, it's me. Sorry I'm late." She took off her coat and hung it in the closet, then put her boots on the mat. For a few moments, she allowed herself to bask in the lovely warmth that came from knowing Tanner had helped her. He'd smiled as if he meant it—as if the rumors about her didn't matter. Just as he had the day Rowan was born, when he'd held her hand and assured her he wouldn't leave.

She couldn't indulge in the sentimental feeling for long, however. Rowan was just starting to wake and she'd want to be fed soon. Laura had been stuck at the bank longer than she'd anticipated thanks to her dead battery, and she didn't have any supper made. She checked her watch. Gramps liked to eat at six sharp. It was just after seven.

Before Rowan tuned up and started crying, Laura hustled to the fridge and took out leftovers from last night's roast beef dinner. Gramps loved meat and potatoes, and it was a good thing because Laura wasn't the world's greatest cook. She'd bought one of those ready-to-bake roasts, microwaved frozen vegetables and managed to boil potatoes, all without burning the house down. She checked a small plastic dish and saw there was only a little gravy left from the packet mix she'd made. Maybe she could add a bit of water to it and it would be enough for Gramps.

She was happy to have him. But trying to be Martha Stewart while he was here was proving to be a bigger challenge than she'd expected. She was sure he'd get that pinched look on his face when she presented him with a warmed-up version of last night's meal.

Rowan was awake and grumbling, so Laura took her out of the seat and held her with one arm while using the other one to take off her little pink coat and hat. Laura ventured into the living room, where she found her grandfather in his favorite chair, watching the end of the six o'clock news.

"Sorry about dinner. I'm getting it now. I had some car trouble."

Gramps was seventy-five and still sharp, but he'd never had to cook or do for himself. With Gram in the hospital for a few weeks with a lung infection, Laura had suggested he stay with her. And she wasn't sorry. She didn't have a lot of family around, and they'd been so good to her since she'd come home. But living with Gramps had its challenges all the same.

"Your car all right?"

"I need a new battery. I got a boost in town that got me home. McNulty's is closed until tomorrow."

"I was hoping to go see your grandmother tomorrow. Since we missed today."

Yes, they'd missed driving into Great Falls. Truth be told, Laura was exhausted. Between being up with Rowan, caring for Gramps, and trying to make ends meet, she was stretched to the limit. Today she'd asked to stay home because she was trying to work on a freelance project she'd taken on. The only reason she'd gone into town was because she'd realized she'd run out of diapers.

In the kitchen, the microwave beeped, indicating the first plate of food was ready. "I'll see what I can do," she promised. "Come on out to the kitchen, Gramps. Supper's on."

She went to the kitchen and swapped the heated meal for the cold one and set the timer again. "Could you put some water on for tea, please?" she asked. "I'd like to change Ro before we eat."

Gramps grunted a response, but he grabbed the kettle and started to fill it. Laura tried to be patient. Gramps had been the one to work and Gram had stayed home, raised kids and looked after her husband. Laura wasn't against that kind of existence, even though these days it was rarely practical. That had been their choice. The downside was that Charlie Jessup had never really had to do anything remotely domestic in his life, and at seventy-five he was unlikely to change. He simply didn't understand why Laura was so incompetent in the kitchen.

Once Rowan was changed, she started to fuss.

Laura made sure Gramps had his meal, but it was increasingly clear that she would not have time to eat before feeding Ro. God, she was tired. She poured water into the mugs to let the tea steep. "Sorry, Gramps," she said, trying to inject some brightness into her voice. "I've got to feed Ro. The tea's steeping, if you don't mind taking out the bag when the timer goes."

"Yeah, fine," he said. "The beef's good, by the way."

She didn't realize how badly she'd needed the compliment until it was given, and her eyes stung with unshed tears. "Thanks," she answered, scooting out of the kitchen so he wouldn't see. She went to Rowan's room. Laura slept in here, too, on one of those blow-up beds with the fold-up frame, since she'd given Gramps her bedroom for the duration of his stay. She sank into the padded rocker and settled Rowan at her breast, exhaling several times to help her relax.

She loved being a mom. And these were precious, precious moments. Laura wished she could stop being so resentful. She resented having to breast-feed in here because her grandfather found it so embarrassing. She resented having to work when she was so exhausted because her maternity benefits were long gone. And while she tried to be grateful for her blessings, it was hard when she went into town and received knowing stares from so many people. They also gave Rowan curious looks, as if expecting her to resemble Gavin.

As far as anyone knew, Laura was a home wrecker. General consensus was she'd been having an affair with Gavin Wallace and Rowan was his child. They'd been high school sweethearts, said the whispers. And the moment she'd come back to town, they'd started up again. And then the worst rumor of all: that he'd been leaving her place the night he had the accident and was killed.

One of these days, she was going to have to leave Gibson behind. Even if she could live with the rumors and whispers, it wouldn't be fair to do that to Rowan, especially as she got older. She wished she could tell everyone the truth, but she couldn't. The only person who knew was her lawyer and Maddy Wallace—Gavin's widow, who'd promised to keep Laura's secret. She had to let it go for her own safety. For Rowan's.

Gavin Wallace was not Rowan's father. And if Spence ever found out that he had a child...

It would be nothing short of a nightmare.

Chapter Two

Laura clicked the mouse one last time and sat back to look at the banner she'd created. She frowned. Something wasn't quite right. The background was beautiful, and the graphic highlighted the client's product perfectly. It was the font, she decided. It needed to be slightly slimmer, and a deeper shade of plum.

So far, the freelance work was paying her bills, but just. Still, it would take time for word of mouth to spread. At least this way she was home with her child instead of having to commute to an office, as she had done during her six-month contract that had ended in December.

Ironically enough, she was still floundering with setting up her own site. She tried to keep her personal details very, very quiet. Plastering her name all over a site made her uncomfortable, and she knew she could decide on a company name, but people still wanted the name of the person they were dealing with. It was hard to advertise and drum up business without a website. Particularly when you were a web designer.

She adjusted the font, felt better, and saved the banner before emailing it off to the client for their thoughts. Then she checked her phone. Damn. They should have left for the hospital half an hour ago. She shut down the computer, dropped the phone into her bag and went looking for Gramps.

She found him sitting on the back deck in a plastic patio chair. It really wasn't a deck, but rather an oversize landing at the top of the back stairs. There was room for one chair and that was it. She pasted on the customary smile. "Sorry I took so long. Are you ready to go?"

"Sure. Been ready an hour now," he said, putting his hands on his knees and pushing himself to standing.

There were times she knew he didn't mean what he said as criticism. It didn't mean she didn't take it that way.

Ten minutes later, they were on the road, and it seemed like no time at all and they'd arrived at the hospital. While he visited Gram, Laura sat in the family waiting room and nursed Rowan. Then she popped into Gram's room to say hello, and left again to get a couple of sandwiches from the cafeteria, as well as some cranberry juice for Gram. The nurses were very good about letting Laura use the kitchen on the floor to make Gram's favorite cold remedy—cranberry juice mixed half and half with boiling water. She always said it soothed her throat and cough and drove out the chill. Laura made a cup for Gram and a cup for herself, as she'd always liked it, too, and a cup of tea for Gramps.

By two o'clock, Laura reminded Gramps that they had to get back to Gibson, as she had an appointment at the lawyer's office. So far Rowan had been contented, so Laura dropped Gramps at the diner and said she'd be back in half an hour to pick him up. The appointment at the lawyer's office was brief. She'd wanted to check on Spence's status. The idea of him being eligible for parole after what he'd done sent a cold chill down her spine and kept her up at night. With Spence having served nearly a year of his three-year sentence, Laura wanted to make sure she kept tabs on the situation.

Like when she really needed to start worrying. She could breathe easy for another few months anyway.

She found Gramps sitting in a booth with a cup of tea and a piece of half-eaten cherry pie in front of him. She'd taken Rowan out of the car seat and held her in her arms, and when she slid into the booth, she settled the baby on her knee, curled into the curve of her arm.

"That didn't take long," he commented. "I'm only half-through my pie."

"Take your time," she said, knowing Gramps was tired from being out all day. She was, too, but rushing him wouldn't benefit either of them. Besides, the food here was better than what he got at home. Unfortunately.

He sipped his tea and took another bite of pie, and a waitress came over to see if Laura wanted anything.

"What can I get you?" she asked.

A hot bath, a glass of wine, and an hour of quiet, Laura thought, but she merely smiled. "A glass of chocolate milk, I guess," she replied. She'd forsaken caffeine months ago, with the exception of her evening cup of tea. Since she'd never been fond of plain white milk, chocolate was her way of getting her calcium.

The waitress returned quickly with her milk and Laura took a long drink, enjoying the cool, sweet taste. She licked the froth from her top lip and settled more comfortably into the vinyl seat of the booth.

"Everything okay at the lawyer's?" Gramps asked, looking up at her over his mug.

"Yes. Fine."

"Don't know why you need a lawyer anyway," he grumbled. "They're expensive."

Didn't she know it. And Gavin had helped her for free, because they were friends. His colleague was giving her a break because of Gavin, but it wasn't free.

"It's complicated," she replied, drinking again. She put down her glass. "Nothing for you to worry about, though. Promise." She smiled. Gramps was gruff, but she knew he worried and cared. He wasn't a fan of her raising her baby alone, but he'd never said a word about Gavin, or the fact that he'd been married. It was as though they'd agreed to not mention it.

He put down his fork. "Laura, are you okay? Really? I'm old and I'm not good for much, but if you need help…"

She melted a bit, her frustration of the last week ebbing away. She touched his fingers with her free hand. "I'm fine, Gramps. I've made some mistakes, but I'm working on getting my life back on track."

"You know how I feel about some of that," he murmured, keeping his voice low. "But you're a Jessup. And you're made of strong stuff. You can do whatever you set your mind to."

Except protect myself, she thought, hating the idea that she could feel so helpless, hating even more that she was scared. Still, the praise made her feel stronger. "Thank you, Gramps."

"Humph," he said, back to his gruff self. But she smiled a little to herself.

Laura didn't notice anyone approaching the table

until she heard the voice that sent shivers of pleasure rippling up her spine. "So, did you end up replacing the battery?"

She swallowed and looked up to find Tanner standing beside the booth, an easy grin on his face.

It would be easier if he weren't so darn handsome. His dark hair was slightly mussed, his blue eyes twinkled down at her and his plaid shirt was unbuttoned at the top, revealing a small V of tanned skin.

She hoped she wasn't blushing. "I did, yes. The guy from McNulty's was kind enough to bring one out and put it in for me."

Tanner frowned. "I would have done that, and saved you the labor cost."

"Thanks, but it wasn't that bad." She glanced over at her grandfather. "Gramps, have you met Tanner Hudson? Tanner, this is my grandfather, Charlie."

Tanner held out his hand. "Sir," he said, giving a nod as they shook hands.

"Tanner's the one who gave me a boost the other day," Laura explained.

"Have a seat," Gramps said. "Laura's always so bent on doing everything herself, but I'm glad there are some people who are willing to lend a hand—even when she won't admit she needs one."

Laura gaped at him. Hadn't he just said she could do anything? Of course. He still prescribed to the old school where certain things were "man's work." Auto repair clearly being one of them.

Tanner slid into the booth beside her, and she quickly scooched over so they weren't pressed together. To her annoyance, he gave Gramps his winningest smile. "Happy to do it. Though from what I've seen, Laura's pretty capable of handling herself."

Gramps gave Tanner a long look, then a quick nod and calmly cut another bite of pie with the edge of his fork.

The waitress came over with a coffee and doughnut for Tanner, and he thanked her with a wink and a smile.

"You're not working out at the ranch today?" Laura asked.

"I had to make a run in to the hardware store. I was going to grab a coffee to go, but I saw you and thought I'd see how you made out after the other day." He shrugged. "At least the weather's improved. Much more spring-like."

He looked over at her half-empty glass. "Chocolate milk?"

She grinned. "What can I say? I'm a kid at heart."

"Speaking of kids…" He peered around her shoulder at Rowan. "Wow. She's cute."

"Thanks." Laura looked down at Rowan and a familiar wave of love washed over her. "She's been an angel all day, so I'm waiting for things to go south really soon. We've been to Great Falls to the hospital to visit my grandmother, and then went to a couple of appointments. Babies have a way of letting you know when they've had enough."

"I bet. Your grandmother—is she okay?"

"She's had a lung infection, but we hope she'll be out of the hospital on the weekend. Gramp's been staying with us in the meantime."

"Laura's been taking good care of me," Gramps said, pushing his pie plate away. He patted his belly.

"That was a good piece of pie. Maybe I should have another."

Laura felt a flush infuse her cheeks. "You're just saying that because I can hardly boil water. I wouldn't let you starve, Gramps."

He grinned and picked up his tea. "Honey, I know that. You got your looks from your grandmother. But you didn't get her cooking skills. That's just a fact."

He looked so amiable that Laura couldn't be mad—though she was embarrassed. Particularly when Tanner chuckled beside her.

Rowan wriggled in her arms and Laura looked down. "We should probably get going soon," she said. "Dragging her from pillar to post today means she hasn't had her regular sleep or feeding schedule. This could get ugly." She aimed a stern look at Charlie. "She has the Jessup temper."

Tanner laughed and Gramps sent her a look of approval. But then Tanner peeked over at Rowan, and Laura suddenly felt uncomfortable. Sure, there was a lot of Jessup in Ro, but Tanner was probably looking for bits of Gavin. He was nice to her, but he probably thought the same as everyone else. Plus, he was connected to Maddy through Cole. And while Maddy and Cole knew the truth, no one else did. Besides her lawyer, they were the only people she'd trusted in all of Gibson, and that was only because her conscience couldn't take it anymore.

Tanner's face remained relaxed and pleasant, though, and she gave Ro a little bounce on her knee. The baby giggled and then shoved a fist into her mouth, sucking on her fingers. A sure sign she was getting hungry.

"Are you almost ready, Gramps?" Laura tried to urge him along. But Gramps had either forgotten the urgency of small babies or was determined not to be rushed, because he shifted in his seat and lifted his teacup. "Just a bit of tea left. I won't be long."

The noises from Ro chewing on her fist got louder and Laura smiled weakly at Tanner as he bit into his doughnut. A familiar tingling started and Laura realized it had been nearly four hours since Ro's last feeding. *No, no, no*, she chanted in her head. But Rowan started to squirm and cry, nuzzling her face towards Laura's shoulder. And when Laura looked down, she was sure her face burned with instant embarrassment.

"Damn," she whispered, staring at twin splotches on her shirt. She'd worn a light blue cotton blouse, and there was no mistaking the wet spots. Sometimes breast-feeding was not completely convenient.

It would be the better part of twenty minutes by the time they paid the bill, she got everyone in the car and they drove home. And if she were alone, she'd discreetly slide to the corner of the booth, drape a flannel receiving blanket over her shoulder and do what was necessary. But Gramps wasn't comfortable with it at home, and she was certain he'd make a big fuss about it in public.

"What's the… Oh." Tanner's voice was soft beside her. Rowan started crying in earnest and people started looking over. To her frustration, Gramps poured more tea into his cup from the small silver pot.

"I can go. If you…that is…"

She shook her head and motioned toward Gramps. Thankfully, Tanner understood.

"I see. Give me two minutes."

He scooted out of the booth and went to the counter. A moment later, he returned with a young, pretty waitress behind him.

"Tanner says you could use some privacy for a few minutes." The words were said kindly. "Come with me."

"You're sure? I don't want to inconvenience you…"

"Don't be silly." She raised an eyebrow and her gaze dropped to Laura's shirt. "The sooner the better from the looks of it."

Laura was pretty practical when it came to nursing, but she had to admit that this moment was pretty humiliating. She grabbed the diaper bag and slid out of the booth. "Thanks," she whispered to Tanner as she passed by him, and he flashed her a smile.

The waitress led her to an office in the back. "This is Joe's office," she said. "But he's not in today, so you won't be interrupted."

"Thank you so much, Miss…"

"Shoot. Just call me Chelsea." She grinned. "My big sister has two kids and believe me, I understand."

She closed the door behind her with a quiet click. Rowan was frantically rubbing against Laura's shirt, and with a sigh, Laura sat on a saggy sofa and got Ro settled.

Several minutes later, she tucked everything back into place. Ro had eaten, burped, and was now sleeping peacefully in the crook of Laura's arm. But Laura was anything but peaceful. Her grandfather was still out in the diner, probably irritated beyond belief at being kept waiting. She really should pack up and get him home.

She was putting the flannel cloth back into the diaper bag when a soft tap sounded on the door. "Come in," she called quietly. She expected it to be Chelsea, so she was surprised to see Tanner poke his head inside.

"Is everything okay in here?"

She laughed. "I'm put back together, if that's what you're asking."

He stepped inside, and she laughed again at the relief that relaxed his facial muscles. "Chelsea mentioned that…" His cheeks colored. "Well. That you might want a different shirt. I went to the department store and bought you something," he said, and she thought he looked rather bashful admitting it. He handed her a small bag.

She reached inside and took out a black T-shirt in what appeared to be the right size. "Chelsea said that?"

He nodded. "Yeah. She's a nice girl. She…well, never mind. She said a medium would probably fit you."

"You bought me a shirt?"

"Well, your other one was… You know."

"Stained with breast milk?"

He blushed deeper.

She sighed. "Tanner, that was really sweet of you. I'm sorry if I was too blunt. I honestly think that once you have a baby you kind of give up on maintaining any sense of dignity. Stuff just happens." The wonder of being a mom was sometimes tempered with a direct hit to a woman's vanity.

He smiled. "Hell, Laura, I was in the ambulance that day. I think that ship sailed a long time ago."

Yes, he had been. He'd held her hand, breathed with her, checked on her progress. Just as any ambulance attendant would have. Except…she vaguely remembered pleading with him to stay with her. She'd felt so alone, so afraid, so…adrift. Without an anchor to keep her steady and hold her fast. And he'd stayed, she remembered. He'd held her hand and encouraged her to push and told her how great she was doing.

Then he'd disappeared. He'd done his job and gone above and beyond, but that was all it was. His job.

Buying her a T-shirt was not his job. And neither was boosting her car or finding her a private spot to nurse her baby. Tanner wasn't just a good EMT. He was a good man, too.

"This really was very thoughtful." She met his gaze. "And I should get out there. My grandfather is probably having a canary by now."

"I actually looked after that, too. He was grumbling, so I told him to head home. I told him I'd bring you along when you were ready." He wiggled his eyebrows. "I hope he didn't lie when he said he still has his license."

"He does. But he only drives in Gibson. Ever since his accident last year, he doesn't like going on the highways or driving in the city."

"Which is why you went to the hospital today."

"Exactly. He's aged a lot since the accident. And he relies so much on my gram that I thought it would just be easier having him at my place for a few weeks."

He must have sensed some hesitation in her voice, because he raised his eyebrows. "And has it been? Easier?"

She sighed. "I wish. I feel pretty inadequate most of the time. Suzie Homemaker I'm not."

"Charlie's old school. Hell, you're supporting yourself and your kid. You can't do everything."

She knew he meant the words to be encouraging, but instead she ended up feeling a familiar dissatisfaction. This wasn't what she'd wanted her life to look like. How had she gotten so off track?

"Anyway, if you're ready to go, I'll drive the two of you home."

Laura swallowed. Gramps was probably put out by the whole thing and now she'd ended up inconveniencing Tanner, too, who probably had things to do. "I'll be right out. I just need to change." She pushed herself up off the couch, but the busted springs meant it took her three tries. By the end of it, she was trying not to laugh, because Rowan was peaceful in her arms and Laura didn't want to disturb her.

"Here," he said gently, and reached for Rowan. "I'll hold her. And I'll turn around."

As carefully as if he were holding glass, he took Rowan and tucked her into his arms. She looked so small there. Small and safe.

Just as he'd promised, he turned his back to her. Laura quickly unbuttoned her blouse, took the tag off the T-shirt and pulled it over her head. It was a little too big, but she was okay with that. The soft cotton was comfortable, and the black wouldn't show any lingering moisture. She wondered if he'd thought of that when he picked it out. She doubted it. Guys weren't generally that astute.

But then, Tanner was different. She'd known that for a long time.

"Thanks," she said, putting a hand on his shoulder. "The shirt's great. Where's the receipt? I'd like to pay you back."

Tanner turned back around, his eyebrows puckered

in the middle. "Pay me back? Don't be ridiculous. It's just a cheap shirt. An emergency shirt." Again the impish gleam lit his eyes. "Come on. My truck's out front."

"Can I ask one more favor?" It was late in the afternoon. Laura had planned to be home earlier, and was tired from the running around. She really needed to put in a couple of hours on the computer tonight. "Could we make a quick stop at the grocery store? I think I'll grab one of those rotisserie chickens from the deli section."

He chuckled, and she sent him a dark look. "Not one word about my cooking."

She took Rowan from him and then swung the diaper bag over her shoulder.

"You're really good to him, you know. He loves you a lot. I could tell."

Laura knew it was true, and sometimes it was the only thing that kept her in Gibson. "He and Gram have been very good to me, too." She wanted to say how grateful she was that they'd never thrown the rumors in her face, but she didn't want to open that can of worms with Tanner. "It's the least I can do. That's not to say I won't try to save my sanity where I can." She grinned. "And save him from an ulcer."

He laughed again and she realized she liked the sound of it. It was happy and carefree, two things she hadn't been in quite some time.

"The grocery store it is."

They were walking through the diner when she realized the car seat had been in her car. "Tanner? I forgot her car seat. Oh no..."

Tanner walked ahead and opened the door. "I put

it in my truck. I don't have a clue how to fasten it in, but it's there."

Relief rushed through her. Gramps fussed and went on about how in his day people simply carried babies on their laps, but she would never do that with Rowan. She needed to be buckled in securely. Safe. Protected.

Laura swallowed against a lump in her throat. Everything she did these days was for Rowan's protection.

At the grocery store, Tanner offered to stay in the car with Rowan while she ran inside. Her daughter was sound asleep, so she left her in the backseat, knowing she'd be perfectly safe with Tanner. In less than ten minutes, she was back in the truck and they were on their way to her place, the interior of his vehicle smelling like roasted chicken.

She and Tanner chatted about the ranch a bit, and she mentioned her graphic design work, which led to explaining what she'd been doing since leaving Gibson after high school. She left a lot of blank spaces, but then, so did he. He didn't mention Cole or Maddy at all, and she knew why.

She wished she could tell him the truth about Rowan's father. But the more people who knew, the more likely it was to get around, and right now that secret was her biggest form of protection.

He carried the grocery bags to the door while she managed Rowan and the diaper bag. When they walked in, Laura discovered her grandfather emptying the dishwasher. She nearly fell down from the shock.

"Gramps!" she said, slipping off her shoes. "You don't have to do that."

He gave his customary harrumph. "Don't know

why everyone thinks I'm helpless. I can put some dishes away now and then."

"I guess I'll get a start on supper, then. You'll be relieved to know I stopped and picked up a chicken."

"Are you staying, young man?"

Laura's mouth dropped open. Had Gramps just asked Tanner for supper? Oh, she hoped he wasn't getting any ideas. Tanner Hudson was the last person she should get involved with. Talk about complicated!

Besides, she was hardly looking for romance. She had her hands full right now.

"Thank you, but I should probably get home."

Laura was surprised to feel disappointment at his refusal, but the last thing she wanted was for him to feel obligated. "You're welcome to, Tanner," she offered weakly, knowing Gramps would expect it. "It's the least I can do for all your help. But if you need to get back to the ranch, I understand."

He rubbed his chin. "I don't need to hurry back. I guess it would be all right."

Oh Lord. Oh Lord, oh Lord. She was actually nervous. Tanner Hudson was going to eat supper at her house. With her grandfather. After seeing her in a mess this afternoon. What on earth? He didn't seem to care a bit about her reputation, either. And there was no way he could have remained oblivious. He had to know about the gossip. About what kind of woman she was... And that had nothing to do with Gavin Wallace and everything to do with her decisions before coming home to Gibson.

Gramps patted Tanner on the shoulder. "Come on in the living room. It's been a while since I've had another man to talk to."

Tanner looked over at her. "Do you need anything?" he asked. "I'm not a complete idiot in the kitchen."

She shook her head. "Thanks, but no. You go. Entertain each other." She gave a self-deprecating grin, glanced down at the chicken and then back at him. "It's not like it'll take long."

He flashed her a smile that felt very intimate, as if they shared a joke. She liked, too, that he'd offered to help, and wondered if he'd said something to Gramps earlier that had prompted the dishwasher emptying, because that was an unprecedented event.

As the men sat in the living room and talked about community goings-on, Laura buckled Rowan into her bouncy seat and began putting together a green salad. She then took out a pretty bowl and transferred potato salad into it rather than simply putting the tub on the table, and placed a paper napkin in a little basket and filled it with buns from the market bakery.

Maybe she hadn't cooked it, but she could at least make the meal look a bit homey.

Just before everything was ready, the baby woke and Laura made a quick trip to the nursery for a change and tidy-up, and then, by some miracle, it all came together.

The table was set, Rowan was playing with the activity bar on her bouncy chair and Laura called the men to supper as she put the carved chicken on the table, along with the salad bowls and butter for the buns.

There was chatter, and the clinking of silverware on plates, and the odd laugh. A lump formed in Laura's throat as she realized this was the nicest meal she'd spent in her house. It had been so long since she'd experienced a relaxed, pleasant atmosphere that she'd nearly forgotten what it was like.

But as Tanner laughed at a story Gramps told, it all came rushing back to her. And it made her both a little bit happy and a little bit sad. She had been lonely for so long.

And that was why, despite the grumbling and inconvenience, she'd offered Gramps a place to stay, she realized. She was *so* tired of being alone.

After dinner, Tanner insisted on helping with the dishes, which didn't take long at all. When they were done, he said goodbye to Gramps and then pulled on his boots and prepared to go.

"Supper was good," he said, standing in the doorway. "Thanks for having me."

"You're welcome. And thanks for being so kind to Gramps. I think he's been a little lost the last few days. It was good for him to have someone besides me to talk to."

"He's a good old dude," Tanner said. "He's pretty proud of you, you know. Says you have gumption."

She blinked back sudden tears. "He's not crazy about me being unmarried with a baby."

"Being a single mom is hard. He knows it. He just wishes you didn't have to do it alone."

"He wishes I'd been smarter."

Tanner studied her for a minute. "Maybe. But I think that's you putting words in his mouth."

He was right. She was pretty hard on herself, and she knew it. And yet Tanner didn't seem to judge. She wondered why.

"Doesn't it bother you?" she asked bluntly. "What they say about me?"

His eyes darkened. "You mean about Rowan's father?"

She nodded, nerves jumping around in her stomach. He was the first person she'd broached the topic with, and she realized that for whatever reason, she trusted him. Oh, maybe not with the truth, but he'd already proved he wasn't about to shun her because of the grapevine.

"It's none of my business," he stated, not unkindly. "And believe me, Laura, after all these years, I know what it's like to have to live with mistakes. And live them down."

"You?" Granted, she'd heard he was a bit of a player, but if that was the worst anyone said about him...

"Right. You were gone for a while, so maybe you don't know. I was married once. For three whole days. In Vegas. The entire town knows about it. My best man at the time wasn't discreet with the details."

She blinked. "You were married for three days?"

"Yeah. Until we both sobered up and she came to her senses. You don't have the corner on mistakes, Laura, and I certainly have no right to judge anyone. So no, what they say doesn't bother me."

He leaned forward and placed a chaste, but soft, kiss on her cheek. "Take care and thanks again for dinner."

"You're welcome. And thank you for everything today." She smiled. "You're starting to become my knight in shining armor."

He laughed. "Oh, hardly. Just being neighborly. Anyone else would have done the same." He raised his hand in farewell and stepped outside. "See you around."

He fired up his truck and drove away, leaving Laura

back in reality again. But it was a softer kind of reality, because for the first time in a long while, it felt as if someone might be in her corner.

And she truly hadn't realized how lonely she'd become until someone walked in and brought sunshine with him. Tanner had said that anyone would have done the same, but she knew that was a lie. She'd been in that parking lot for a good half hour with the hood up before he came along to help. Others had passed right on by.

It was just too bad that Tanner Hudson was the last person she should get involved with. Even if Maddy was gracious enough to understand, she knew the town of Gibson never would.

Chapter Three

Tanner threw a bale of hay down the chute and followed it with two more. The physical exertion today was his form of therapy. If he had to hear one more time about how much his parents loved Maddy and how happy they were that Cole was dating her and how adorable her twin boys were, he was going to lose it.

He got that the whole family was happy that Cole had fallen in love. Hell, he expected there'd be an engagement announcement any day now, and he was truly happy for his brother.

But this whole love-fest thing just made Tanner feel more like a loser every day. The last thing his ex Brittany had said to him was that he'd be a joke for a husband. And seeing Cole and Maddy and his mom and dad so thrilled only seemed to highlight the fact all the more.

Tanner was good for a good time. Girls loved him for that. And that was it. The problem was, it wasn't enough for him. Not anymore.

His bad mood persisted through the chores, over breakfast, and late into the morning. He decided to saddle up Bingo and go for a ride, using the excuse of checking on the calves in the east pasture. Maybe the fresh air and open space would help put him in a better frame of mind.

He loved the scent of the young grass, the spears yellow-y green in their newness and the buds that were getting plump on the trees, nearly ready to leaf. Spring was a relief after a particularly harsh winter, and since that last snowfall earlier in the month, the weather had turned mild. Even if they did get a late season storm, there was a sense that the weather had truly turned a corner and there were warmer, greener days ahead. Spring was a time of year Tanner usually loved.

But this year he was filled with a nagging dissatisfaction. As he walked Bingo along the fence line, he sighed. It was only partly to do with Cole. He found himself thinking about Laura quite often, too.

Maddy had seemed to mellow out where Laura was concerned. Maybe that was because she was happy with Cole. But Tanner had noticed the sideways looks aimed in Laura's direction the other day at the diner. If he noticed, he was certain she did, too. People looked at her and saw a woman who'd had an affair with a married man. But where was the blame on Gavin? Just because he was dead, it was as if he was blameless.

Sometimes people put their faith and emotions in the wrong people. He knew that as well as anyone. They shouldn't have to pay for it their entire lives.

Dinner at Laura's house a few weeks ago had made one thing clear to him. Laura Jessup was in sad need of a friend, and no one would go near her. It was as if they were afraid they'd catch something. He hadn't seen such a lonely person in a very long time. Talking to her grandfather, Charlie, had enlightened him a fair bit. She never had friends over. Rarely went out anywhere other than errands. No wonder she'd clung to his hand the day Rowan was born. How afraid she must have been, facing that alone. When he'd given her that cheap T-shirt at the diner, she looked so surprised, so touched, that he wondered how long it had been since anyone had done anything remotely thoughtful for her. Her grandfather had also been concerned, but reserved. It wasn't hard to see he disapproved of the situation, even though he loved her.

Tanner turned Bingo around and returned to the ranch a little less on edge, but still unsettled about the whole situation. It wasn't just Laura. His life seemed stuck in place. What was he going to do, live with his parents forever? Satisfy himself with short-term hook-ups now and again? That whole scene was getting old. Maybe having a place of his own would be a start.

When Tanner returned to the house, he found Maddy there, helping his mom paint the back deck while the boys napped. Cole and Dad had driven down to Butte to look at some stock. Tanner was at loose ends, so once he grabbed a sandwich for lunch, he hopped in his truck and drove into town. And through town, and west. There was no sense kidding himself. He was going to see Laura. Just to see how she was making out. If there was anything she needed.

He pulled into the driveway and noticed things he'd missed the last time he was here. Like how the paint was peeling on the railing of the front step. A piece of soffit was missing from the roof overhang, and one corner of her eaves trough needed to be repaired, too. Nothing major, but little things that needed fixing that she probably couldn't do herself. Or could, but because of her situation, didn't have the time or money.

She came outside the moment he got out of the truck. He lifted a hand. "Hi," he greeted, and a lot of the restlessness he'd felt all day dissipated at the sight of her. She wore a pair of faded jeans and a cute white top, and Rowan was on her hip, dressed in a pink flowery outfit. They made a sweet picture.

"Hi, yourself. This is a surprise."

"Yeah. I'm not here at a bad time, am I?"

She shook her head. "Come on in. Rowan's up as you can see, so I'm spending some time with her and I'll go back to work when she's napping again."

"Work? What are you doing?"

He climbed the steps and she opened the door, leading the way in. "I'm working on a web design for a new client. I only had a six-month contract at the last place, and with Ro being so little, day care's not an option. This gives me some freedom and some income."

"That's smart." He followed her inside. Just like the other night, the place was spotless. His respect for her grew. She might not have much, but she took pride in what she did have. "What about Charlie?"

She laughed. "Oh, he's been back home for about a week. And thrilled about it. Gram's still taking things slowly, but at least he's eating better. Do you want some coffee or tea? I have both."

"Naw, I'm good."

"Then what are you doing here, Tanner?"

He floundered for a moment, and then decided he might as well tell her the truth. "I guess I found myself thinking about you a lot, and wondering how you are. Wondered if you, uh, needed anything."

Her gaze turned sharp. "You feel sorry for me, is that it?"

"No!"

She sat at the kitchen table, so it only made sense for him to do the same. "Not sorry, per se," he continued. "Well, crap. I have no idea how to say this in a tactful way. I'm a guy. And this is kind of like navigating a minefield."

She put Rowan on her lap and handed her a plastic ring with big, colorful keys on it. The baby shook the keys and a little giggle bubbled out of her mouth. Tanner couldn't help the smile that tugged on his lips. The kid was so darn cute. A few short months ago she'd been tiny, all arms and legs and thin cries. He couldn't help feeling a strange sort of attachment, knowing he'd helped bring her into the world.

"You want to ask me about Gavin."

He met her gaze. She was looking at him evenly, but as though she was bracing for whatever he was going to say or ask. "Not exactly. I just noticed the other day that…" He hesitated.

"Just say it, Tanner. I've heard it all."

He sighed. "That's what I mean. I noticed you're kind of, I don't know, set apart. People treat you differently. Not mean, just…"

"Polite. And look at me sideways like they're trying to figure something out."

"Yeah. And I wanted to say I'm sorry about that. And if you need anything, you can give me a shout. I don't judge. If Rowan is Gavin's…well, it took two of you, and until someone walks in your shoes, they really don't know about a situation."

She smiled softly. "That sounds very insightful. Is this about you or me?"

"Maybe a little of both," he admitted. "You didn't

know me when we were all kids. I'm a few years younger than Cole, and you were gone when I ran off to Vegas with Brittany. I screwed up, but people have long memories around here. It's like they've never made a mistake in their lives."

"So what is this? Are you championing an underdog? Or maybe throwing things back in their faces? Proving they're right about you, that you're a screw-up by hanging around with the wrong kind of woman?"

"Ouch."

A wrinkle formed between her eyebrows. "Sorry. That was me being superblunt again. I'm the first one to admit I have a bit of a chip on my shoulder."

Despite the harshness of her words, he could tell she'd asked an honest question, and he thought hard about how he would answer. Was he doing this to prove a point? Because if he was befriending her in a way that was anything less than genuine, that made him no better than anyone else.

"No," he said softly. "That's not what I'm doing. But that was a really good question to ask, Laura." Rowan dropped the keys on the floor. He leaned down, picked them up and handed them to her. He received a toothless grin as his reward. "It's more that I know how it feels, and it's wrong. I'm not afraid to be your friend if you need one. You *and* Rowan. I was there when she was born. It was a big moment."

He didn't expect tears to gather in her eyes. It made the blue depths even bluer, and his heart stuttered a little. He wondered what the heck he should do now.

"Sorry," she murmured, and reached for a paper napkin to wipe her eyes. She took a few deep breaths.

"Honestly, you're the first person to say that since Gavin. That you're my friend, that is."

"I'm sorry," he said, and he meant it.

She cuddled Rowan closer. "Tanner, I can trust you, right?"

A little ripple of warning slid through him. No one asked that sort of question unless they were planning on revealing something personal. But then, he'd just said he wasn't afraid to be her friend. So he nodded, holding her gaze. "Yeah, you can trust me."

"Because there are only two people in Gibson who know the truth besides my lawyer. One is your brother. The other is Maddy Wallace."

Gavin's widow.

"This has to do with Gavin?"

She nodded. "Okay, here goes. The baby's not his, Tanner. Gavin was a good friend, but nothing more. He was married. I would never get involved with a married man. I've made a lot of bad decisions, but that's not one of them."

Tanner sat back in his chair. On one hand, he felt a surge of relief knowing she'd never slept with Gavin. But on the other, he was completely perplexed. If their relationship had been nothing more than friendship, then why didn't she set the record straight?"

"I don't understand," he said.

"You want to know why I let everyone think otherwise."

"Well, yes!" He frowned, leaning forward again and resting his elbows on the table. "Laura, you know that people think you two had an affair. That Rowan is his. You're deliberately letting that happen, and letting them make you an outcast. Why would you do that?"

"Because the truth is worse than the lie," she said quietly. "And as difficult as it is for me, it's in Rowan's best interest, and I have to put her first."

Which really didn't explain anything.

Rowan started fussing, so Laura got up and put her on her shoulder. Tanner noticed again the difference in coloring. Laura's hair was wavy and a gorgeous auburn shade of red that he knew most women coveted and few came by naturally. Her skin was creamy white with a few light freckles, her eyes a clear summer blue. Rowan, while having the same pale skin tone, had perfectly straight dark brown hair, and her eyes were blue, but not the same vibrant shade as her mother's. Gavin's hair had been brown like that, too, but he couldn't remember the man's features well enough to know if there was any imagined resemblance.

To the townspeople, the implication was enough. He knew that people often saw what they wanted to. Such was the power of suggestion.

So if Gavin wasn't the father, who was? And why was that truth so much worse than letting the world think Rowan was Gavin Wallace's?

"Tanner? Let's go into the living room. She's got a bouncy seat in there that she loves. It's almost nap time anyway, and I can explain a little better."

He followed her into the living room and sat on the sofa while she settled Rowan in the little chair and gave it a bounce. The girl's face lit up and she smacked at the toys on the activity bar in front of her.

"Best thing I bought for her," Laura said, smiling. "She loves it and it's saved my sanity more than once. Now that she's awake longer through the day, she gets bored." She sat in the chair to the right of him and let out a big breath. "I suppose I need to elaborate a bit, don't I?"

Did she? Was it really any of his business? He thought about what it meant to be a good friend. He had friends, but Cole was really the guy he was closest to. And even then, there were things his brother didn't know. Tanner totally understood how it felt to want to keep the darkest parts hidden away. Curious as he was, he knew how he had to answer. "Tell me only if you want to," he said. "You don't owe me any sort of an explanation at all."

"And that's very generous of you. And surprising."

"Like I told you before, I've had a few moments that are not my finest. I don't judge."

She smiled at him then, a soft curving of her lips that reached in and grabbed him right by the heart. It was sweet, and perhaps a bit vulnerable—something he hadn't seen in her up to this point. Except for one moment, last December. When she'd had a particularly nasty contraction and she'd reached out for his hand in the ambulance. She'd looked so scared and yet so trusting.

"You know, I'm starting to believe that's true," she whispered.

There was a long pause, and then she put her hands on her knees. "You've been nothing but kind to me, and I trust you. So here's the truth, leaving out some names if that's okay with you."

"You can tell me as much or as little as you like."

She looked relieved. "The truth is, up until last spring I lived in Nevada, in Reno. I was working for a small graphic design company and my roommate tended bar. Through her, I met this guy and we went out a few times. He was really handsome and charming, and he said he was in sales." She laughed bitterly. "Pharmaceutical sales. God, I was so dumb, so naive," she said, giving a bitter laugh. "Anyway, it was a bit of a whirlwind thing. But then he said he was being transferred to a new territory for a few months and he ended it. A few months later, he came back, and he was still handsome, still charming…but something felt off. I couldn't put my finger on it, but there was an edginess to him that hadn't been there before. A… hardness. I think I knew I should end things, but I told myself I was imagining it. I ignored all my instincts."

Tanner didn't like where this was going. At all. "Did he hurt you?" he asked gently.

Her eyes clashed with his, but she shook her head a little. "No, not like that. He never laid a hand on me. He came into my work and wanted to start up where we left off, and I fell for his charms all over again. I let him stay with me at my apartment until he found a new job. But after a few weeks back together, I knew it wasn't what I wanted. I didn't feel safe, though I couldn't explain why. A few times, some guys showed up at my door, and I knew he wasn't honest about who they were. All my internal alarms were ringing and so I decided I needed to break it off."

Tanner hadn't realized he'd been holding his breath until she paused and he let it out. "And then what happened?"

"The day before I was going to do it, the cops came and arrested him. He totally lost it when they showed up, and God, it was so ugly. He was charged with violating his parole, assault and battery and possession of a controlled substance. I had no idea about the drugs.

Turns out that transfer? He wasn't working. He was in prison." Her normally sparkly eyes had dimmed, her lips thinned to a straight, disapproving line. "He wasn't a pharmaceutical rep at all. He was dealing. To kids. And I was too blind to see the signs. By then it was too late."

Tanner didn't say anything; he simply sat quietly while she composed herself. He knew what it was like when you found out the person you thought you loved turned out to be totally different. Though at least Brit hadn't been a felon. Just...not who he thought she was.

"The baby's his?" he finally asked.

She nodded miserably. "When they left with him, he looked right at me and said he'd be back, just like last time. Not to worry, he'd come find me when he got out. The way he said it...it made my blood run cold. It wasn't reassuring. It was a threat. If he knew about Rowan..."

Tanner looked from her to the sweet baby bobbing in the bouncy chair. The two of them weren't his, but damned if he didn't feel protective of them just the same. "He'd come after you both."

She nodded again. "Yeah. I had to give a statement to the police and I found out a lot about his past. I was so stupid, Tanner. So blind. I believed every lie he fed me. How many kinds of idiot could I be? And then to get pregnant..."

The agony in her voice was real. "I'm pretty sure you didn't mean for that to happen," he said quietly. He got up and moved to the end of the sofa so he was closer to her, and he reached out and put his hand on her knee. "Listen. Remember that marriage I mentioned? I was totally in love with this girl Brittany from Lincoln. She and a couple of girlfriends moved to Vegas, and I thought I'd surprise her one weekend. It was crazy." He decided to leave out some of the more sordid details about the weekend activities. "By the end of it, we'd gotten married at a chapel on the Strip."

"Oh."

"Yeah. Oh. And when I asked how long it would take her to pack up and come home with me, she laughed. She had no plans to leave. She loved it there. She loved the lights and the excitement and the party. She certainly didn't love me. It was all a crazy, fun adventure to her."

"And you were dead serious."

"You betcha." He smiled wryly, trying not to think of the moment when Brittany had all but fallen over laughing at him. "We all make mistakes. And I guess now I understand why you haven't set the record straight. Because you'll take the gossip if it means keeping your daughter safe."

A tear slid down her cheek. "Oh, damn. I spent enough time crying. You'd think I'd be over it by now." She rubbed the tear away. "It's such a relief to actually tell someone, and I think it's made me super-emotional. Maddy only knows the bare minimum and no details. I couldn't stand the thought of her thinking Gavin had cheated on her any longer. He loved her so much."

"But it's rough on you."

"It's worth it if Rowan stays safe."

"Damn, Laura. Why not move somewhere else, where no one knows?"

Once more she looked into his eyes, and he saw shadows there.

"The only way I could get this house was if Gramps and Gram cosigned the loan, and that was before all the rumors. There's no way I'll get financing for another place, not with the little bit of freelancing I'm doing. And I'm having a hard time building the business because I don't want to put my full name on anything. It'll make it too easy to find me, you know?"

"So you're stuck."

"Yep. I mean, I grew up here, but it doesn't mean it's not awkward."

Awkward was putting it lightly. "Gavin was helping you, wasn't he?"

"Yeah, with some of the legalities. And he did the legal fees for the house pro bono. His partner's been keeping me updated on Spen…on my ex's sentence."

She sighed, looked down at Rowan. The bouncing had stopped, and Tanner saw that each blink of Rowan's eyes was slower than the last.

"I feel like I'm spinning my wheels." Her shoulders were slumped a bit as she rested her elbows on her knees. "I want to start over, but it's hard to do when you want to remain invisible. At least with the contract work, my name was kept out of it. But if I'm going to freelance, I can't stay anonymous. Even if I'm careful, it's not hard to find the trail."

"Too bad you can't change your name," he replied, half joking. "Then he'd be looking for Laura Jessup and not Laura someone else."

A crazy, ridiculous, ludicrous idea flitted through his brain.

No. She'd never agree and besides, it was a dumb idea. He kept hearing Brit laugh and say how he wasn't husband material. Maybe not, but perhaps he could be friend material. No one else was stepping up to give Laura a hand. The only one who had was gone, and she had no one to be on her side.

Plus, he was tired of living at home. This could be beneficial to both of them.

"Laura, how open are you to harebrained schemes?"

She lifted her head, chuckled softly. "Why? Do you have one?"

Something twisted in his gut, in an oh-my-God-are-you-really-going-to-ask way. His palms started to sweat and his breath caught. He'd said the words once before in his life, but this time it was different. This time it wasn't for love. So why was he so tied up in knots?

"I just might. And you're going to be tempted to say no, but hear me out."

Her eyebrows pulled together in a puzzled look.

"Laura," he said, not quite believing what he was about to say. "I think we should get married."

Chapter Four

Laura started laughing. Marry Tanner? That was the most ridiculous thing she'd ever heard. "Oh God," she said, between breaths of mirth. "You shouldn't even joke about that."

He was chuckling, too, which was why his next words surprised her even more. "I'm actually perfectly serious. I've wanted to move out of the house for a while now. And if you married me, you could be Laura Hudson. Laura Hudson could set up her own business in that name and not be so easy for this guy to find."

Her laughter died in her throat. She was starting to think he meant it. Her face went hot. Sure, Tanner was good-looking. Extraordinarily so, but she hadn't really thought of him in a romantic kind of way. For a moment, an image flashed through her mind—of her and Tanner doing things that married couples do. Her face burned hotter.

"Tanner, I… I mean, you and me…"

He seemed to understand what she was getting at. "Laura, I'm not talking about a *real* marriage. It would be in name only, of course. We hardly know each other."

"My point exactly." She exhaled a relieved breath.

They were, at best, friends. Their contact had been limited to the ambulance ride to the hospital, running into each other and chatting on a few occasions in town, and the events of the last few weeks. Sure, she liked him well enough, but she wouldn't be roommates with someone she knew so little of, let alone husband and wife.

Husband and wife.

He leaned forward, put his elbows on his knees and peered into her face. "You said you were hesitant to put out your shingle online because it made you too visible. Even if you use a company name, your contact info is going to be listed somewhere. When you register your website, or fill out business forms for taxes and stuff."

All true, but it wasn't as simple as a different last name. "Tanner, it's not like it would be impossible to figure it out, even if I did change my name. There'd be marriage records to show that I was once Laura Jessup."

"Maybe," he conceded, "but it would make it more difficult. And if you're married, chances are that even if this guy did find you, he'd probably think that the baby was, well, your husband's."

"Yours," she said, the word echoing in the strangely quiet room.

"Yes."

Silence fell. He'd hit her squarely where it hurt— her daughter. Her top priority was protecting Rowan. It was why, after all, she let the town of Gibson collectively assume that the baby was Gavin's...even though that made her an adulteress and a home wrecker. But this was different. This was marriage. A wedding. And she wasn't sure what Tanner wanted to get out of it. There must be something. There was no way it was a purely altruistic move.

Good gracious, was she actually considering it?

Of course she wasn't. Harebrained was a great way to characterize the idea. She'd made enough mistakes over the last few years; she wasn't too keen to compound them by marrying a stranger just so she could change her name.

She got up and walked to the window, looking out over the backyard. The grass was greening up, but there were dry, bare patches where the ground was hard and unyielding. Laura sighed. Yes, she had her own place, but it wasn't much. She kept it clean, but it was hardly better than the lousy apartments in Reno. Rundown and unloved. Funny, she was starting to think of herself in those terms, too.

Marrying Tanner was a stupid idea. She'd just keep on doing what she was doing and figure it out somehow. She always did.

"Tanner, I appreciate the offer, but I don't need to be rescued. It's a crazy idea and I think it would be a disaster."

"Why? I like you. And I think you like me." He smiled at her. "We'd be roommates, that's all. No funny business, I promise."

She frowned. "If you want to move away from the ranch, do it. There's nothing stopping you. You don't need to live with me to do that. You're a grown man."

He paused, and then nodded. "That's true." He frowned a little. "Can you sit down, please? You're making me nervous standing up there."

His voice actually sounded as though he wanted to

have a serious conversation, which at this point seemed so surreal it was laughable. No one did marriages of convenience anymore. She certainly didn't. When she eventually said her "I do's," she wanted to mean them.

An ache settled in her heart. That day might never come. She didn't have a whole lot of faith when it came to romance. Now she was a single mom, which made relationships even more complicated.

Laura sat on the sofa, crossing her hands primly on her knees.

"Laura," Tanner began, "I have my own reputation to live down in this town. My three-day wedding in Vegas is still talked about. There's always been speculation about it and I have never said anything because…well, my mom always taught me that a gentleman doesn't talk about a lady. So the consensus seems to be that I'm not serious about matrimony. The truth is, I was the serious one. She wasn't. I didn't come to my senses and want the marriage annulled. She did." He hesitated. "I asked her to come back here with me and she laughed in my face and told me I was the kind of guy girls wanted a fling with, but not marriage."

"If this is your sales pitch, it needs work," she replied dryly.

He gave a little huff that might have been amusement at her witty response. "The point I'm trying to make is that this would be purely an arrangement to get you out of a bind and to get me out of a house where I'm surrounded by—" he made a face, as if tasting something bad "—people who are in love and *show it all the time.*"

"If you're looking for a roommate, why even bring

marriage into it? This isn't my grandparents' generation. People actually live together. Even boys and
girls." She rolled her eyes. At least she could still find
a little humor in the situation.

She'd lived with Spence, because she'd been a dumb
idiot who'd had her socks charmed off. As well as vari-
ous other articles of clothing.

"Because the marriage part is what gives you the
freedom to put your business out there. We could do
it quietly, at the courthouse, and down the road, when
we both think it's time, we divorce. Nice and quiet
and friendly."

He did have a point. And she was longing to get a
site built and start taking on more clients. Still, marriage was incredibly drastic. "You're crazy."

"You'd be saving my reputation, too. I'm starting
to get tired of the Good Time Charlie label."

"Don't you think your rep would be resurrected
when we divorced? I mean, if I were nuts enough to
go along with this stupid idea." She shook her head.
"Tanner, do you even want to be marriage material?
Or care what the town thinks of you? Your reasons are
flimsy at best, so it makes me think there's something
more to your offer."

TANNER WAS QUIET for a few beats, and then he pushed
his hands against his knees and straightened. She was
right. It was a crazy idea and if he wanted to move
out, he could. He didn't need to get married to do it.

It was something else. It was the fear in her eyes
when she mentioned this "Spence" guy. She was afraid
of him and Tanner suspected she had a real reason to
be, if the creep was serving jail time. He liked Laura,

and she was struggling after having made some bad decisions. The simple truth was, he wanted to help. Even if it was temporary, if standing in front of the justice of the peace or a judge meant she could have some measure of protection, he was willing to do it. If he helped her, he'd feel that he was doing something important. Meaningful. He couldn't deny that he felt a strange responsibility toward her and her daughter.

"Laura," he said softly, "I'm not looking for love, and I'm not looking for a real marriage. I was burned once before. Is it so wrong that I feel terrible that you have to deal with this? I know what it's like to have everyone look at you sideways."

"So you're doing this entirely out of the goodness of your heart? Out of charity?"

"Are you too proud to take it? Not everyone likes to accept help." He expected she'd had to swallow a lot of her pride over the last year. Maybe she was tired of it. "If not for me, do it for Rowan."

"You realize that the idea of offering me the protection of your name seems very...well, it's straight out of one of those historical novels my gram likes to read."

He grinned. "Some would call it chivalry."

She raised an eyebrow. "Some would call it antiquated. And an affront to feminism."

He went to her and put his hand on her shoulder. "Sweetheart, my mama always taught me that feminism means the right to choose whatever path you want. You can choose what you want to do now. And there is no shame in choosing something that makes your life a little bit easier and safer for your child. I can't think of a better reason, actually."

Laura blinked. "That's what my mom used to say to

me, too. That it was about owning your choices. I've made some horrible ones, and I don't want to leap into another, you know?"

"Then let me leave it with you. Just think about it. Yes, it's unorthodox. And it's for sure not what you planned, but it could be a solution."

He got up to go. There was no sense banging on about it. Either she'd take him up on it or she wouldn't. And perhaps he was completely crazy to even offer. It seemed like a no-brainer, that's all. When someone was in trouble, you stepped in to help. Sure, this was kind of extreme, but it was also really simple. Never mind that the thought of her ex made his gut clench. Whatever he'd done had to be pretty significant for her to want to be invisible and let everyone think the worst of her.

She walked him to the door. He was on the front step when her soft voice stopped him. "Tanner?"

He turned and looked at her, standing there in the doorway. Her hair curled around her shoulders in dark red waves, and her eyes were clear and soft, perhaps a little sad. She didn't smile. She looked resigned.

"Thank you," she said quietly. "For offering to rescue me. First Gav, now you…well, even if it's a dumb idea, the fact that you offered shows me there are still good men in the world. It means a lot."

"Hell, Laura, you don't need to be rescued. You've got a spine of steel. You couldn't have dealt with the last few months if you didn't. Either way, the offer's still open."

"It's too much." He started to protest, but she raised her hand. "I know, it's only temporary. But it's too extreme."

A cry sounded through the open door; Rowan was awake and complaining. "I'd better go," she said, taking a step back. "See you around, Tanner."

"Bye."

He waited until she shut the door before he went to his truck. He thought about her all through the drive home. Thought about how pretty and sad she looked—except for when she looked at her daughter. Then her face was contented, happy and beautiful. He thought about the tiny house and the little things in need of repair, and wondered how she'd manage on her own. Thought about the man she spoke of and wondered how dangerous he really was. And Tanner thought about his own life, and how long he'd been holding back his real feelings of discontent because there was nothing to be done about them.

The ranch was a family operation and he was needed there. He knew it and it wasn't even that he resented it. It was more of a general feeling that he wanted something more. Something meaningful. Opportunities for that were slim in a town the size of Gibson. Particularly for a rancher with no formal education beyond his EMT certification. Maybe he couldn't make a difference to a lot of people, but maybe he could to one. Well, two. He smiled, thinking of Rowan's soft, dark hair.

When he arrived back at the ranch, he saw Maddy's car out front. She'd be there with her twin boys and she and Ellen, Tanner's mom, would be talking about recipes and all sorts of other domestic things. He thought again of Laura and how she'd admitted she wasn't much of a cook. Maddy was a town darling, and Laura was a pariah, even though she hadn't done what everyone thought she had.

He cut the engine but stayed in the truck, frowning as he surveyed the front yard, everything neatly trimmed around the front porch and a velvety carpet of grass surrounding the property. It wasn't that he begrudged Maddy any happiness. God knew she'd had a rough time, losing her husband. But her life was coming up roses, and Laura was scared...and alone.

It didn't seem fair.

Instead of going inside, he walked to the pasture just west of the barn where the newest calves frolicked about on long, gangly legs. There was something about them that he gravitated toward. They were so cute and unencumbered and playful.

Carefree.

Tanner rested his arms along the top of the fence and watched for a long time, trying to remember the last time he'd felt such youthful exuberance. He suspected it was probably before that fateful trip to Vegas when he'd had his heart stomped on and then handed back to him with a smile. Yes, that had made him grow up in a hurry.

Now he was just tired. Tired of the bar scene, tired of the label that had stuck to him, tired of spinning his wheels.

Laura had asked him what he would get out of such an arrangement. The truth was, marrying her would take a lot of the pressure off him. Pressure to live up to the single man reputation, the opposing pressure to settle down and the pressing need to get away from home and find his own place to live. And if marrying Laura—even for a short while—accomplished that, and kept her and her baby safe, as well? It seemed like a win-win in his book. Love didn't need to enter the equation.

A couple of calves approached the fence to investigate, and he put out his hand, wondering if they'd venture close enough for him to touch. One did, and he scratched the spot between his ears and rubbed his hand along the soft jaw. There was just one problem, of course. Laura thought his plan was nuts. Probably because it was. He was also pretty sure he had no idea how to change her mind.

He'd need to think of something else. With a sigh, he turned away from the fence and toward the house. He couldn't stay away from his family forever.

Chapter Five

As the evening meal ended, Tanner cleared his throat.

"Uh, I wanted to bring something up with you guys and see what you think."

Cole sat back in his chair and folded his arms. "Are you still thinking of buying that bull from Wyoming?"

"This isn't to do with the ranch. At least, not directly." His mom, Ellen, was clearing the table, but Tanner reached out and put a hand on her wrist. "Mom, sit for a minute, okay?"

Their father, John, hadn't said anything up to this point, but Tanner saw one thick eyebrow go up, just a tick. His opinion mattered most of all. John had had the least to say after the Vegas debacle. And he rarely said much at all, which meant that when he did speak you knew it was important. He'd built his whole life around the ranch and had a certain outlook on life. Including what a man did and didn't do.

Tanner was sure his father would have something to say if he knew his son had proposed to Laura Jessup.

Ellen sat back in her chair. "What is it, Tanner?"

He glanced around the table.

"I think it's time I found a place of my own."

Cole frowned. "You do?"

Tanner nodded. "Hell yes. Come on, Cole. You and Maddy are a big deal, and I bet it won't be long before those boys'll be here all the time. You're the real head of this place now and that's how it should be. And I'm a big boy. I probably should have moved out a long time ago. It's just been convenient to stay."

Ellen patted his arm. "Honey, I'm sure no one wants you to feel pushed out."

"I don't," he assured her, though he wouldn't say that he often felt like the odd man out. He knew she—and Cole—would feel badly about that. "I'm a grown man, Mom. Living at home. I kind of want my own place."

"Good," John said.

"Good?" Tanner met his father's gaze. Maybe Ellen hadn't been speaking for everyone.

"A man has to make his own way. You need to figure out what you want, Tanner. And I'm not sure you're going to do that living at home. A little independence can be a very good thing."

That wasn't what he'd expected from his father at all. "Thanks, Dad."

"Of course I'll still expect you bright and early in the morning. We still have a ranch to run."

Of course. Figuring out what he wanted was all well and good, as long as the work got done first. But then, it wasn't any different from what he'd expected, was it?

"Any idea where you'll go?" Cole asked, putting his empty coffee cup on his dessert plate.

Tanner knew where he'd like to go. Despite the poor cooking skills, the little house that Laura had bought was perfect. Maybe he should have suggested room-mates first. What an idiot he'd been to propose. He could have helped her with expenses, at least. Instead he'd come up with the cockamamie idea about marriage. He'd laugh, but then he figured his folks would want to know why he was laughing, and there was no way he wanted to explain his impulsive proposal.

"I don't know yet," he replied honestly. "I'll have to look for a place in town, I guess. Or buy a place."

"Wouldn't you need some savings for a down payment?" Cole asked, chuckling a little.

It annoyed Tanner that his brother assumed he had no money. "I've got enough put aside. But I don't want to buy right away. Not until I'm sure where I want to be."

The silence around the table told him he'd surprised them all.

"I've been saving for a few years," he said, shrugging. "You've been paying me ranch hand wages, Dad, and giving me room and board. I haven't spent it all."

There was a glint of respect in his father's eyes, and Tanner welcomed it.

"You really want to do this?" his mom asked.

Unless he was mistaken, there was a sadness in her voice. He'd be the first of them to leave home, though most parents would be thrilled that one of their grown sons was getting out. He nodded. "I really do. I know the ranch is a family operation, but at some point we have to grow up and do our own thing, don't you agree?"

Ellen laughed. "You say that, but I bet you'll still eat most of your meals here and bring your laundry home."

Warmth flooded him at the affection in her tone. He felt a bit guilty for his dissatisfaction, because there was no doubt in his mind that he was loved. "I'd be an idiot for choosing my own cooking over yours," he said, pushing away from the table and standing. He leaned down and gave her a peck on the cheek. "Thanks, Mom. And Dad."

Cole stood, too, and grabbed the coffee cups from the table. "Face it, little bro. You're just looking for some privacy."

Tanner frowned, his eyebrows pulling together. "You know, Cole, I'm not getting anywhere near as much action as you think I am."

The kitchen fell oddly silent. "Gee, Tan," Cole said into the quiet. "I was just teasing."

Tanner shoved his hands into his pockets. "I know that ever since Vegas you've found it hard to take me seriously. And I played in to that, because I didn't want everyone to know the truth about what happened." He shook his head a little. "Oh, the wedding details are about right. But it wasn't all a lark. I was in love with Brit and I didn't want anyone to see how badly she'd hurt me. So I pretended to be a bit of a rebel and a ladies' man until the label stuck. The last thing I wanted was pity. This was just easier. But it's not who I really am. I thought that at least my family understood that."

Ellen's face creased with concern and even his dad's eyes widened with surprise. "Tanner," he said, his voice deep and sure, "you're a damn fine worker and a good man. You've never given us any reason for embarrassment, so if this is what you want, we're behind you."

He wondered if his dad would say the same thing if he knew about the proposal to Laura.

"Yeah, sorry, bro," Cole added, contrite. "I was just teasing, but I guess I hit a nerve."

"Sometimes people aren't what they seem on the surface," Tanner answered, watching his brother. According to Laura, Cole and Maddy knew that Gavin wasn't Rowan's father. "Sometimes people try to protect themselves by deflecting the truth."

Something flickered in Cole's eyes. Tanner was tempted to let Cole know that he also understood Laura's situation. In fact, he probably knew more about it now than either Cole or Maddy. But it had been told to him in confidence, and he would keep it to himself.

"I'm going out for a while," he said, knowing the alternative was sticking around here and getting stuck in front of the television. Right now he wanted some fresh air and room to breathe.

SEVERAL DAYS LATER, Laura couldn't stop thinking about Tanner's ludicrous suggestion.

She sat back in her desk chair, the casters rolling along the floor. The chair was comfortable enough, though hardly ergonomic. Still, the corner of her bedroom that she used as a home office was cozy. Particularly with a soothing cup of mint tea and an almond cookie from the pack she'd bought at the market. Only one—she was making them last.

As proposals went, Tanner's was hardly romantic. He'd been kind and, well, sexy, though she was pretty sure that was unintended. Tanner Hudson would sound sexy reading the darn phone book. No, his proposal had been just shy of a business proposition.

That had to be the only reason why she couldn't get it out of her head. Because from a purely business standpoint it actually kind of made sense.

Work was slowing down. She was building a website right now, but it was basic, and in another day or so it'd be finished. She should be spending this time building her own site. Drumming up her own business. But every time she thought about registering her domain, or filling out the proper tax and registration forms, she got a horrible twisting sensation in the pit of her stomach.

It was fear. In principle, hiding behind Tanner's name would make her a coward, and she didn't want to be that person. In practical terms…hell, she'd often thought that if she could just change her name she could breathe a lot easier.

Could they do it? It would be in name only; he'd said so. She'd become Laura Hudson. Not, she determined, Mrs. Tanner Hudson. The only thing that would change was her last name. And the fact that she'd have a roommate.

A roommate who she knew would also kick in with the expenses. There was that to consider, too. Even if she shouldered the mortgage on her own, someone to help with groceries and the light bill would be a huge help.

Of course, maybe Tanner wasn't interested anymore. It had been totally impulsive. And if he was, they'd have to lay out some ground rules right off the bat. Including how long they intended for the fake marriage to last.

She'd done a lot of crazy things in her life, but this one might just take the cake.

Before she could think better of it, Laura picked up her cell, and then realized she didn't even know his phone number. She was contemplating marrying the guy and she didn't even have his number in her darn phone. She laughed to herself, a soft sound of disbelief, and shook her head. When the best solution she could come up with was a wedding to a virtual stranger, things had really gotten out of hand.

Later, after Rowan was up from her nap, Laura dressed her in a cute little sweater and bonnet and made the drive into town. She was trying to cook for herself more, finding it cheaper than grabbing a meal at the diner or something prepackaged. Her efforts were dismal at best; she'd burned the stir-fry and discovered charred broccoli smelled horrible, and she'd undercooked the breaded chicken breast she'd attempted, leaving it crispy on the outside and gelatinous in the middle. But she wasn't giving up yet. She'd found a few recipes that looked simple, and she had a list of ingredients to buy. Laura hoped keeping the recipes simple translated to being easy on the wallet, too.

She had Rowan in a Snugli carrier and wheeled the grocery cart in front of her, adding a few packages of ground beef, a small tray of chicken thighs and a couple of pork chops from the meat department. Some people watched her curiously while others didn't seem to know she existed. It wasn't until she'd made it all the way through the store and was finishing up at the bakery section that she crossed paths with Tanner.

Something rushed through her, something that put her on alert. It was pleasure, she realized. She was happy to see him. And from the way his smile lit up his face, he was glad to see her, too.

"Well, hello." Tanner grinned and gave a polite nod. "Oh my gosh, Laura. I think Rowan gets bigger every time I see her."

Bonus points for complimenting the baby right off the bat.

"She certainly does," Laura replied, disgusted with herself for being so elated. She really didn't get out much, did she?

"How've you been?" Tanner asked. He leaned a little closer. "Any progress on the business?"

She shook her head. "I'm still trying to figure that one out." He didn't need to know how little work she was bringing in now.

She noticed the plastic container in his hand and smiled. "Glazed doughnuts?"

He chuckled. "I have a real thing for doughnuts. I love the cakey sugared ones at the diner, and my mom makes awesome chocolate ones. But then there are these kind, too, the puffy, yeasty ones with the sticky glaze. I swear I can eat six before I realize what's happening. They just melt in your mouth."

She thought back and remembered him getting a doughnut that day at the diner when she'd been there with Gramps. "So you have a doughnut addiction," she mused, grinning. "That's a pretty big vice you've got there, Hudson."

He raised one eyebrow. "I know. I've tried to find a Doughnuts Anonymous meeting, but they're scarce."

She laughed outright. When was the last time someone had teased and made her laugh like that?

"What about you?" He looked at her expectantly. "Any vices?"

"French fries," she said without hesitation. "Crispy, hot, salty French fries."

"Yum."

"Right?"

Tanner looked down at Rowan once more and unless Laura was mistaken, a look of tenderness passed over his face. The more she came to know him, the more she was sure that Tanner Hudson was a good man. Her experiences hadn't jaded her to the concept that there were a few of them still out there.

"I'd better not keep you from your shopping," he said, taking a step back. "I just came in for a midday pick-me-up. I'm apartment-hunting this afternoon."

He truly was determined to move out. A momentary flash of panic darted through her body. Maybe she'd lost her chance. It seemed he was serious about getting out on his own and it wasn't something he'd simply made up so his proposal would hold water. That was reassuring.

Laura quickly took things into account. He liked doughnuts. He was a handsome, hardworking guy, low maintenance, practical, but fun. Maybe she'd be stupid to let him slip through her fingers, even if it wasn't a "real" relationship. If she left it any longer, he'd find himself a place and the window of opportunity would close.

"I'm almost done," she found herself saying. "Do you want to grab a coffee to go with those doughnuts?"

"Sure, why not?"

He said it so easily. As though it didn't matter a bit that he was being seen with her. Even if he knew the truth, no one else did. Yet Tanner didn't seem to care. She doubted he knew how much she appreciated that.

It was a beautiful day, so instead of coffee Laura added a bottle of lemonade for herself to her grocery order and checked out. "Why don't we meet by the library?" she asked, digging out her wallet. "We can sit on one of the benches and enjoy the fresh air."

"Sounds good to me," Tanner replied. "I'll go grab a coffee to go with my doughnuts."

Laura sighed in relief as she wheeled the groceries to the car and put them in the trunk. Tanner was generally so solicitous that she'd half expected him to offer to help carry her groceries and then she'd have to refuse. But he hadn't, and she liked him more for it. Chivalry was nice, but it was also good to feel independent and capable and perhaps respected for it. Humming softly, she fastened in Rowan's car seat and drove the block and a bit to the library. When she pulled in, Tanner was already there, holding a brown paper cup in one hand and the doughnuts in the other. She chuckled a little and wondered how many of the sweets he'd eat with his beverage.

It took a minute to get the diaper bag and the lemonade and then put Rowan on her shoulder, but she did it. Rowan perked up, pushing one pudgy hand against Laura's shoulder and looking around with bright, inquisitive eyes.

"You always have your arms full," Tanner commented. "Maddy says she has huge biceps from lugging the twins around." It was no sooner out of his mouth than he looked stricken. "Oh, heck. I shouldn't have said that."

"Why not?" Laura led the way to the crushed gravel path. "I don't harbor any hard feelings toward her. We've made our peace, Tanner. Plus she's going out with your brother. You can talk about her. It doesn't bother me in the least."

"It's just, well, a little awkward."

She shrugged. "The perception of it is for sure, but it's not so bad. She knows that Gavin and I were just friends." She smiled a little. "It's everyone else who is all weird about it."

"Don't you ever wish you could set the record straight?" he asked, falling into step beside her.

"Of course. But then I look at Rowan, and I think that the longer I can keep assumptions where they are, the better."

They found a bench and sat down. Tanner stretched out his legs and sighed. "The sun feels good."

It really did. The warmth of it bathed Laura's face, while a light breeze whispered over the skin of her arms. Both of them wore simple T-shirts—Tanner's brown with a crew neck and hers a navy V-neck. She settled Rowan on her lap, then opened the lemonade bottle.

"Cheers," he said, tipping his coffee cup.

She laughed again, loving how being with him was so fun and easy. "Cheers." She tipped the neck of her bottle and then took a refreshing, tart drink. "Ahhh. That's good."

She bounced her right knee a little, keeping Rowan occupied, but the baby was so happy to be in the sun and fresh air, with all the bright colors of grass and sky and trees and flowers, that she sat perfectly contented.

"She likes it outside," Tanner said, putting his coffee down carefully and reaching for the doughnuts.

"She does. I wish our backyard was in better shape. We've gone out a few times, but it's not like this. Not with the nice grass and the flower gardens."

"You should put out some planters. Maybe a bird feeder or two. I bet she'd like that."

Laura nodded but looked down. She'd love to, but it always came down to money. And the fact that she wasn't making any. And that she needed to get her business officially up and running. Put out some proposals. She clenched her teeth, knowing what she had to ask. Feeling stupid. Feeling...desperate. And yes, even a little cliché. Screw that. A lot cliché. *Ugh, ugh, ugh.*

He held out a doughnut.

She took it, the sugary glaze clinging to her fingers. "Thanks," she murmured, and dutifully took a bite. Light, sweet, melt-in-your-mouth delicious. She licked the extra glaze off her lips and swallowed.

"Looks like Rowan wants some, too," he said, giving a small nod.

Rowan was leaning toward Laura's hand, her eyes focused on the doughnut and her little lips smacking. Laura laughed, put a tiny bit of the sweet on her finger, and placed it on Rowan's lips.

The happy smacking that followed made them both laugh. And that was when Laura knew what she had to do. She'd started a new life for herself and her daughter, but she needed to disappear better. And to do that, she needed Tanner.

"Tanner, about your suggestion the other day..."

He crammed the rest of his doughnut into his mouth and her confidence faltered.

It took several seconds for him to chew and swallow. "What suggestion? Do you mean..."

Her heart pounded ridiculously. "About us getting, you know...married. In name only, of course."

The smile slid from his face, and she was certain he'd changed his mind.

He licked off his thumb, turned a little on the bench so he faced her. "You've reconsidered?"

"When you mentioned apartment-hunting, I realized you must have been serious about wanting to get a place of your own. I actually considered asking you to move in as a roommate. That in itself would be a help…"

"Financially," he finished. "But not with the other problem. Of wanting to stay unfindable."

After a pause, she replied. "Yeah. So maybe we could be roommates who share a last name? It's not exactly ordinary, but it could work." Lord help her, did she actually sound a little hopeful?

His gaze held hers for a long minute. She noticed the deep blue of his irises, the black pupil, the little darker ring of blue that seemed to outline the color. This was riskier than she'd admit to him, because he was incredibly attractive and kind to boot. She'd have to be very careful not to let herself get personally involved. Stay friends. Ignore any inconvenient attraction that cropped up.

"You're sure? I mean, I'm still game if you are."

She glanced down at Rowan and a familiar wave of love washed over her. "For Rowan," she said softly, then looked up at Tanner. "I would do anything to protect her. You didn't see his face when he said he'd find me. I believe him. And whether or not it makes me weak…well, I'm scared, Tanner. If this means I can provide for my daughter and stay out of his way, I'll do it."

There was one thing that nagged at her. To be honest, there were several things they needed to talk about if they went through with it, but the one that she'd wondered about most was the reaction of the town. "You do realize you'll be the subject of gossip. That people will think you're crazy. I'm used to it by now, but you're not."

"After the Vegas incident, they'll probably say we deserve each other." He gave a self-deprecating huff, but then took her hand in his. "It'll be okay."

"Remind me again why you're doing this? Because marrying someone is a pretty big favor, you know? It's not like boosting a car or picking up a loaf of bread, or—"

"Shh," he said, giving her fingers a squeeze. "Maybe I don't like how you've been treated. And it's not like marriage holds a whole lot of meaning for me anymore, you know? I'm not going into this with any illusions. It's a contract between friends."

It sounded so cold. And yet there was relief, too. Why couldn't marriage be a simple contract for them? They didn't need to go into it with a lot of emotion and sentimentality. They could define it however they wanted.

"So we're going to get married?"

He nodded. "Let's do it." Then he rubbed his hand over his hair and laughed.

"What?"

"I just realized I have no idea where to start."

"Me, either," she replied. "I suppose we have to apply for a marriage license. Book a judge or justice of the peace or something. Tell our families."

Tanner's eyes caught hers. "Yes, we should do that. Are you up for it?"

The very idea made her stomach feel weightless. Somehow she dreaded telling her grandparents more than facing down Maddy and Cole, and Mr. and Mrs. Hudson.

She swallowed tightly, then nodded. "Let's iron out some details first, though, okay?"

"Good idea." Tanner closed the lid on the last remaining doughnuts, the plastic snapping together and getting Rowan's attention. Her hands waved up and down at the sound. "I have to get home and help Cole finish up for the day. But maybe later? I'll clean up and come over to your place, after Rowan goes to bed. We can work out the finer points then. How does that sound?"

Scary as hell.

"That's fine. We'd better get home, too. I have groceries in the car and I should get some of them in the fridge."

They got up from the bench and walked the short distance to the library parking lot. They were nearly to her car when Tanner slowed, and she looked back to see what the hold-up was.

His brows was knitted a little. "Laura, do you... I mean...hell. Do you want an engagement ring?"

That he asked made her heart hurt. Tanner Hudson was a genuinely nice guy. And despite the very platonic nature of their relationship, he was standing there looking like an unsure schoolboy asking if she wanted an engagement ring.

Maybe this was a mistake. But then again, Laura had accepted long ago that she would probably never have a real wedding and husband. Things didn't tend to work out that way for her. That didn't mean she didn't believe in them, though. To wear a ring when it wasn't real seemed almost sacrilegious.

"It's okay, Tanner. I don't need a ring." She smiled at him, wishing she could be happy and not feel this sadness weighing her down. "I'll see you later tonight, okay?"

"Okay."

He looked relieved. And not for the first time, Laura berated herself for the choices she'd made that put her in this position.

Chapter Six

By the time Tanner turned into Laura's driveway, the sun was almost down and his bad mood had moderated slightly.

Granted, he'd been edgy ever since he'd gotten back to the ranch. Laura had taken him by surprise today. He'd already decided that proposing had been foolish and silly, and of course she wouldn't say yes, which was why he'd started looking for his own place. But once she'd started talking he couldn't possibly tell her he'd changed his mind. Besides, it didn't have to be a huge deal. Like he'd said—it was nothing more than a contract between friends. The problem came with the realization that they'd probably have to keep that part quiet, which complicated things a fair bit. Were they going to have to pretend to be in love? He thought of her thick, coppery hair and blue eyes and the way she smiled, and knew pretending wouldn't be that difficult. A blessing and a curse.

Laura had turned on her porch light and he looked at it for a few seconds after he killed the engine.

He'd had had a few moments of panic since leaving her this afternoon. And then, after dinner, Cole had started in on the "going out yet again" thing and how

Tanner was never home. His parents said nothing, but he'd felt their agreement with Cole, real or imagined. In response, he'd snapped back that this was why he wanted his own place, and he'd gone out the door with his sour attitude leaving a bad taste in his mouth.

He was going to get married.

He blew out a breath, wishing he felt the same sort of happiness that Cole experienced with Maddy. Tanner had, once. It had been his biggest mistake. He shouldn't expect happiness now. He *didn't* expect it. He was looking to help someone who needed a hand. To do something that mattered more than shoveling cow shit and fixing fences. That was all this was.

If they married, a woman in a tough situation would be better able to provide for her daughter. As reasons went, it was good enough for him. And everyone else could take their opinions and shove them. He was sick to death of them.

Tanner got out of the truck and shut the door. It really was peaceful out this way, he realized. The air still held that spring-like scent, and he could hear peepers nearby, from either a little brook or some resting water. The sky was a peachy-lilac color, striated by wisps of pearly clouds. He took a moment and breathed deeply, trying to stop the merry-go-round in his head. He and Laura would figure this out, one detail at a time.

He climbed the steps slowly, lifted his hand and knocked on the door.

When Laura opened it, all the practiced words flew out of Tanner's head. She looked…wow. She'd dressed up. Nothing fancy, but she wore a pretty dress with little flowers on it that fell to just above her knees.

The gravity of what they were going to discuss struck him again.

"Hi," she said, and her cheeks flushed as she stood back and held open the door. "Come on in. Rowan's already asleep."

"Thanks." He entered and took a few moments to pull off his boots and put them by the door. She walked over to the fridge and the skirt of her dress swayed with each step. Tanner's mouth went dry.

"I made some iced tea. Do you want some?"

"Sure." His voice came out on a croak and he cleared his throat. "That'd be nice."

She turned back from the fridge with a glass pitcher in her hand. "I can't cook, but I can manage tea, hot or cold." She put it down and reached for a glass. "I guess you should know that right away if you haven't figured it out already. I'm not much of a cook. Sweet or plain?"

"Plain's fine," he said, and she poured and handed him the glass. Their fingers brushed and he got that nervous swirling in his gut again. Which was stupid. It hadn't been this way this afternoon in the park.

Laura poured her own glass of tea, added sugar and stirred it. Then she looked up at Tanner and took a shaky breath. "Are you having second thoughts?" she asked.

"Are you?"

She shook her head. "No fair. I asked you first."

He was, but he didn't want to admit it. It wasn't about wanting to or not, but more to do with the seriousness of the situation. He was glad of that, actually. That neither of them was being flippant about it.

"No," he replied.

"Okay. Let's go in and talk, then."

He followed her into the living room. A lamp was already lit in the corner, chasing away the twilight and making it cozy and welcoming. Laura sat in a chair, leaving him the sofa. It told him a lot that she didn't sit with him, but chose to put some distance between them. Keeping it businesslike. Which might have worked except for that dress. He'd never seen her in one before. When she crossed her left knee over her right, he caught a glimpse of a small tattoo just below her ankle bone. From where he sat, it looked like a hummingbird.

There was a lot he didn't know about Laura Jessup.

She picked up a pad of paper and a pen from the end table and clicked the top, preparing to write.

He got the feeling he was about to fill in a lot of the blanks.

LAURA FIGURED THE only way to get through the evening was to treat it like a business meeting. Otherwise she'd be liable to lose her focus and get all sentimental or weaken and not go through with it.

A contract. That was all this was. They needed to discuss terms and plans and timelines, and to keep it straight, she needed to write it all down.

"So," she began, forcing her voice to come out calm and even. "The first thing we should do is pick a date and work from there."

"The sooner the better, I suppose." Tanner sipped his tea and smiled encouragingly.

"It's May. We're headed right into prime wedding season, and most officiants are probably booked.

Would you like me to check into it and find the first available date?"

He looked shocked for a moment, and then the pleasant expression returned to his face. "Yes, that would be great."

"Surely we can find something in the next month. Why don't we work with that presumption, and then we'll shift if we need to? Does it matter if it's on a weekend?"

He was quiet, so she looked up from her paper. His expression was slightly blank, so she nudged, "Tanner?"

"It doesn't matter. One day is as good as the next."

"Good." She made a note on her paper and looked up again. "I'm assuming you'd like to tell our families before we go to the county office for a license. I was thinking this weekend we could get it over with and then Monday go fill out the paperwork. Do you think your parents will be around for that? I can call my grandparents tomorrow and set something up. Gram's still slow getting around, so they'll probably be home most of the weekend."

"I suppose telling them should be first on our list." He frowned.

"And probably the hardest part," she said. "And we should talk about how we're going to present it. Are we going to be honest about why we're doing it? Or are we going to, you know, act like it's real?"

Tanner stared at her for a long moment. "I don't know," he answered cautiously. "What do you want to do?"

She sighed and her shoulders slumped as she sat back in her chair. "I honestly don't know. I keep thinking how disapproving my grandparents will be if we tell them it's in name only. They're old-fashioned. They already think our generation doesn't take marriage seriously enough."

"They'll still be disappointed down the road, when we divorce." Tanner ran his finger along his lower lip. "The question is, which would be worse for them? Or harder for you? Now or later?"

She didn't answer. "What about your folks? What do you want to tell them?"

He pursed his lips. "I don't know. I don't know if we could sell it to them, you know? Your grandfather has at least seen us together, and we could let him draw conclusions. But I'm not sure that'd work with my family. I'm not sure they'd believe we fell in love."

He almost stumbled over the words, and she realized the idea had him scared to death. It was probably just as well.

"Plus, Maddy and Cole will ask questions," she said.

"And Mom and Dad…well, they know the rumors, Laura." His eyes were wide and honest as he looked at her. "Maybe it would be better to tell them the truth."

Laura shook her head as her chest tightened. "No, Tanner. Too many people know already. I know your parents are good people, but the more who know, the greater the chance of something slipping. Maybe we can tell them we've been seeing each other in private. With the baby, we might be able to sell that notion."

Tanner nodded slowly. "That might work. I go out a lot, just to get out of the house. And I mentioned wanting to move out recently. But, Laura…" His gaze touched hers. He was so serious right now. It was strange seeing him this way, and not the happy, smiling guy she normally encountered. There was something incredibly alluring about Tanner Hudson when he was being responsible and somber.

He sighed. "With my family, I think you're going to have to be prepared for some push back. Because of my history, because of yours. It shouldn't matter, but there'll be questions."

"Like if we want to rush into this. If you're ready to be a father. If I'm the kind of girl you want to be saddled to for life." It hurt to say the words, even though she knew it was true.

"Possibly. And for you, too. I have a terrible track record with marriage. They'll want to know if you're sure you know what you're getting into."

"So we shouldn't count on them for unqualified support."

"They'll come around. But probably not right away. I don't want to see you get your hopes up."

She chuckled, a dry, humorless sort of laugh. "Hopes, Tanner? I gave up on high hopes a long time ago."

The sad truth of that settled around them. "I'm sorry," he said, and he sounded as though he absolutely meant it. It was an odd moment to feel so incredibly close to him, but she did. What a pair they made. Romantic failures, both of them. Poor judges of character. And yet this time, in this one instance, she felt she was one hundred percent right to trust in him.

"So," he said quietly, "that just leaves deciding what to do about, uh, living arrangements."

She swallowed. "Well," she said, lifting her eyes to his, "you might as well move in here. You can have the bedroom and I'll sleep in with Rowan, like I did when Gramps was here."

Tanner frowned and shook his head. "Laura, you're not sleeping on a blow-up mattress. You should have the bedroom. Maybe we can move Rowan's crib in there and I'll sleep in her room."

Laura thought of the pastel-painted walls, the frilly curtains and the decals of flowers and hearts she'd stuck on the wall in lieu of more expensive decorating. "Really? It's not quite your style."

"Then we'll get you a new bed. Put it in that room so you have a decent place to sleep."

"It should be a single bed. It's cheaper and that way Rowan can move into it when she's older and we're—"

She stopped abruptly.

"Divorced," he finished.

"This is the strangest conversation," she admitted. "Tanner, are we crazy?"

"Probably," he agreed. "But it's our business. No one else's."

"You can move in as soon as you like," she said. "Either before or after the…the wedding."

"Okay." He tapped his foot lightly, and she realized he was nervous. It made her feel better somehow, and made her like him even more. Tanner was a good man. But he was also human, and she didn't feel like a complete failure around him. That was something very different from other relationships, including the one between her and Gavin, which had been friendly. Still, there'd been a superiority there that neither had spoken of, but existed nonetheless. Gavin had been married, with twin babies, and a career as a lawyer. What had Laura achieved since high school beyond screwing up? Sure, she had a career, but it barely paid her bills and her personal life was a disaster.

"If we've covered the basics, I guess I should go," he said, putting his hands on his knees. "You probably want to get to bed soon."

It was barely past eight-thirty. "You could stay a while if you wanted," she suggested. "If we're going to live together, we'll have to get used to being in the same room from time to time."

"Of course. We're friends. That doesn't have to change at all." The words were the right ones, but there was a strain around them, too. As if he was trying to convince her—or himself.

"Do you want to stay and watch TV for a while? I usually watch one of those procedural dramas from nine until ten. Or we could watch something else if you want."

"That sounds fine to me." He patted the cushion beside him. "You can sit over here if you like. I don't bite."

The sofa did afford a better view of the television. She got up from her chair and picked up the remote, then sat carefully on the cushion, leaning against the padded back and crossing one leg over her knee. There was no sense pretending this was easy. Maybe it would be better if they just got everything out in the open. "This is kind of awkward, isn't it?" she asked.

Tanner grinned. "Aw, it'll just take some practice. If we're going to be convincing, we should get used to spending some time together. It'll be expected."

"I suppose you're right. I hadn't thought of that."

He turned to face her as she clicked the button

on the remote to turn on the TV. "You can trust me, Laura. You know that, right?"

Did he realize he'd said those words to her before? She found herself locked in his gaze, his earnest eyes searching hers. It had been in the ambulance on the way to the hospital, and she'd started to panic. The pain had been getting intense and she was scared and feeling alone and as though everything was out of control. Tanner had been there beside her, focused on her face as the contraction seized her body, reassuring her that her baby was fine and everything was going to be okay. "You can trust me, Laura," he'd said, holding her hand. "Everything is going to be just fine. Breathe."

It was hard to breathe again, but for a very different reason.

"I want to believe that," she said. "You've been the first person to really be a friend since…"

"Since Gavin died."

She nodded.

"Do you miss him?"

The sound from the television provided some background noise, but she heard only Tanner's voice, saw only his face. There was no judgment or condemnation written on it. It was the strangest thing.

"Is it wrong to say no?" she asked, feeling her cheeks heat. "I mean, not in the way you mean. We dated in high school, and he was a good man, but we were truly just friends. I felt terrible when the accident happened, of course. He was far too young and with such a nice family. But I wasn't in love with him, Tanner. Our past gave us a connection and I knew he was a good man. That was why I asked for his help. Not because I was still…no."

She squeezed Tanner's fingers. "Thank you for asking, though. You're the first. Because of the rumors, I haven't felt entitled to any grief, you know?"

He squeezed her hand back.

"Tanner?"

"Yeah?"

She licked her lips nervously. "There's something else I want you to know."

"Okay."

"Even if I'd had feelings for Gavin, I wouldn't have acted on them. I've made a lot of mistakes, but I'm not the kind of person who would cheat, or be The Other Woman."

"I know that," he said easily. Just like that. As if there was no question at all of her integrity.

And then he smiled at her, and her heart gave a definitive thump in response.

She slid over on the sofa and turned to face the TV. Roommates. That was all they were going to be. Maybe they'd have to pretend otherwise for a while, but she'd simply keep reminding herself that it was fantasy. That it was all for Rowan and her future.

The opening theme of her show began and she pretended to concentrate on it while Tanner relaxed and hummed along a little with the music.

They were going to do this. It was the craziest thing she'd ever done. And if it worked out, the smartest. Just as soon as they got to the county office and got the license.

Chapter Seven

Tanner's palms were sweating as he and Laura made their way from the truck to the front steps of her grandparents' small bungalow. The yard was plain, but it was well kept, with the grass freshly mowed and a few pots of red flowers sitting on the gray-painted wooden stairs. Charlie and Patricia Jessup were in their seventies, but it looked as though they were still more than able to care for the property.

Laura was dressed in neat pants and a flowery spring top. Very casual, but pretty and feminine, too. She'd dressed Rowan in a romper that was red and white and ruffled beyond reason. Right now Rowan was perched on Laura's arm as they neared the door. Laura looked as nervous as he felt. But they'd agreed that telling her grandparents first would be easiest.

Patricia came to the door and opened it in welcome. "Laura, dear!" Tanner noticed the older woman's skin was pale, but her eyes twinkled out a welcome. "Goodness, Charlie told me you'd been spending time with a young man." Her smile widened. The knot in Tanner's stomach tightened.

"Gram, this is Tanner Hudson. Tanner, my grandma Patricia."

"Ma'am," Tanner said, taking off his hat.

"Oh, no need for ma'am." She flapped her hand at him and opened the door wider as they ascended the steps. "Come in, you two. I baked some cinnamon rolls this morning and I put on a pot of coffee."

"You didn't need to do that," Laura chided. "You should still be resting."

Patricia chuckled. "I'm not dead yet. Besides, those cinnamon rolls aren't a speck of trouble. And they're your grandpa's favorite."

The inside of the house was so clean Tanner was sure they could have eaten their rolls off the shiny floor. The décor was old-fashioned, but welcoming, and Patricia led them straight through to the kitchen. Patio doors led to a small back deck, and the door was open and the screen pulled across so the warm breeze wafted in, bringing with it the scent of grass and the sweet aroma of some sort of flowering shrub.

Charlie came around the corner. "Well, now. I knew there had to be some occasion for cinnamon rolls. Hello, sweetheart." He grinned and went right to Laura, planting a kiss on her cheek. Then he touched an arthritic finger to Rowan's nose before holding his hand out to Tanner. "Nice to see you again, Tanner."

"Thank you, sir."

"Sit down, you two. Tanner, what do you take in your coffee?"

"Just a little cream, thanks."

"Are you having coffee, Laura?"

"Maybe just half a cup," she said, and Tanner glanced over at her. He knew for a fact that she wasn't drinking much caffeine because she was still breastfeeding. The idea itself made a warm blush crawl up his chest, thinking about the way her full breasts filled out her top. He needed to stop that sort of thinking. Truth was, he was sure that she only agreed to the coffee because she was anxious about this afternoon and wanted to be as accommodating as possible.

When everyone had a cup of coffee and a plate with a warm roll, Laura settled Rowan on her knee and smiled weakly at Tanner. She wanted to get it over with. As the moment stretched out, her eyes seemed to plead with his. She wanted him to be the one to speak up.

His heart pounded in double time and he took a deep breath. He put his mug on the table. "Mr. and Mrs. Jessup, we asked if we could visit today because we wanted to tell you some news."

Charlie's gaze narrowed slightly, but an easy smile remained on Patricia's lips.

Different phrases rushed through his head, all jumbling together as he struggled with what to say next. "We, uh…that is, since Christmas…" He coughed and started again. "You probably know that I was one of the EMTs in the ambulance the day Rowan was born."

"Yes, of course," Patricia said, smiling encouragingly. "And she's so precious, isn't she?"

"She is," Tanner agreed. "The thing is, since then, well, Laura and I have been seeing a lot of each other. The other night I asked her to marry me and she said yes."

Charlie's keen eyes darted from Tanner to Laura and back again. Tanner noticed that Laura's cheeks held twin red spots and that she was focused on something on Rowan's collar instead of looking up.

"Laura?" Charlie said her name gently, and Tanner saw her steel herself, then lift her head and smile at her grandfather.

"Tanner's been so good to me," she said, her voice sweet and soft. "He's kind, and considerate, and gentle. And he doesn't mind that I'm not a very good cook." She laughed lightly, and Tanner admired how she was able to make a small joke. It somehow made her explanation seem more authentic. The compliments already made him feel a little awkward. He also felt guilty for lying, and imagined her guilt was far worse. After all, Charlie and Patricia were her family, not his.

Though his was up next.

"Oh, sweetie," Patricia said. "I'm so happy for you, if this is what you want. That sweet little girl should have a daddy."

Ouch. He knew that would hit Laura right where it hurt, but she only smiled at her grandmother and ran a hand over Rowan's dark cap of hair.

"You're sure this is what you want?" Charlie asked, his gaze sharp and assessing. The blush on Laura's cheeks brightened, and Tanner stepped in.

"Laura's a strong, capable, kind woman. I'm a very lucky man, Mr. Jessup."

"I seem to recall telling you not to hurt my girl," Charlie said, his lips a thin line as he stared at Tanner.

"Grandpa! When did you do that?"

"The day I was at your place for dinner and we were in the living room," Tanner replied, holding the old man's gaze. "And I have no intention of hurting her, sir. Just the opposite. I want to take care of her."

"I can take care of myself," Laura said acidly.

He looked at her and raised his eyebrows. "Of course you can. That's obviously not what I meant."

Of course she could look after herself. But he figured the couple they were trying to convince would appreciate the sentiment.

Patricia did for sure. "Will you stay at the family ranch, then? And does this mean you're not going back to work, Laura?"

He let Laura field the questions. "We'll live at my house, and Tanner will drive to the ranch each day. And I most certainly am going back to work. I'm going to increase my business and work from home. That way, I can help support the family and still be with Rowan."

Her grandma smiled. "I've always felt a girl needed a skill. You just never know when you might be on your own. Good for you, honey." She turned to Tanner. "Tanner, this girl's going to keep you on your toes."

"I'm counting on it," he replied, picking up his fork.

"One more thing," Laura said. "Neither one of us wants anything big. We've booked a justice of the peace for three weeks from today."

"That's the third week of June. Oh, what a lovely time for a wedding. But can you be ready that soon?"

"It'll be a small civil ceremony, Gram. It's what we want."

Tanner wished he could take Laura's hand. He wondered if she was thinking about a big church wedding with a white dress, flowers and all the trappings women seemed to like. Maybe he should have asked if she wanted that. It just seemed more expedient this way. Besides, he'd have a hard time making his vows in a church knowing they weren't for real.

"Are we not to be invited, then?"

There was disappointment in Patricia's voice, and

he gave Laura a short nod. Surely, they could each have a few people present. He'd want Cole to be his best man, or at least his witness for the official documents.

"Of course you're invited," Laura replied, her voice light with what he thought sounded like relief. "You're my closest family."

"It'll just be you, and a few from my side," Tanner said. "We haven't picked a location yet, but we'll let you know as soon as we do."

The conversation relaxed for a while then, and they ate cinnamon buns and sipped coffee and talked about Rowan's latest milestones and Patricia's recovery from her illness. After they'd been there an hour, Rowan started to fuss and Tanner knew they should get on to the ranch and get the rest of the day over with. Laura disappeared to change Rowan's diaper and Tanner thanked the Jessup's for the hospitality, trying not to feel like a fraudster. It wasn't until they were outside on the step that Charlie put his hand on Laura's arm.

"Girly, are you sure you know what you're doing?" He said it in a low voice, but Tanner heard. He knew Laura had to answer this one herself, and wished she could be spared having to. However, they'd decided to do this and it had been with the full knowledge that difficult conversations were part of the package.

"Gramps," she said softly, patting his hand, "it's about time I started making some smart decisions in my life. I have Ro to think of now, too. Tanner's a good man and I'm happy when I'm with him. I know I'm doing the right thing."

Charlie's sharp eyes softened somewhat. "You take care of our girl, you hear?" He aimed this command at Tanner. "She's one in a million."

"Yessir, she is," Tanner agreed. "Thank you for the coffee and rolls, Mrs. Jessup."

She held out a plastic container. "I packed some for you to take home," she said, pressing them into his hand. "Let us know the details, now."

"We will."

They walked back to the truck, and Tanner felt both a rush of relief that it was over and another wave of anxiety since they still had to face the Hudson family. Laura buckled Rowan into her car seat and then got in the passenger side, letting out a deep breath as Tanner started the engine.

"One down, one to go," he said encouragingly, while inside he felt like a man about to start the long walk to the gallows. Maybe he should tell them alone, but then they'd wonder why Laura wasn't there.

And to be honest, it felt right that they face their families together. It was what real married couples did and they needed to give the impression of being a real couple, didn't they? Unless...

"You're sure you don't want to tell them the truth?" he asked, half hoping she'd changed her mind.

"I keep asking myself the same question," Laura answered as they turned out of the drive onto the road. "But the fewer people who know about Spencer the better, Tanner. I keep coming back to that."

"You can trust my parents, you know. And Maddie and Cole already know."

She sighed. "Can we talk about this later? Maybe someday down the road? But not today."

He heard the stress in her voice and felt badly that he'd added to it. "Okay," he replied, heading east toward the Hudson ranch.

They were halfway there when Rowan started crying.

"Is it nap time or something?" he asked, his nerves starting to fray. He was edgy enough without adding the shrill cry to the mix.

"Yes, probably. And she's hungry. I knew I should have fed her earlier, but my grandfather is so uncomfortable with me nursing…."

Tanner's jaw clenched. "And you probably don't want it to be the first thing you do at my parents' place, either, huh?"

"I should have, you know, expressed enough for a bottle." Her cheeks were bright red.

Tanner tried a smile. "The practicalities of having a small baby," he offered. "As a paramedic, I've heard a lot of moms say that once you've had a baby, modesty kind of goes out the window."

She gave a relieved laugh. "Yeah, that's about right. Modesty is sometimes a real luxury. Moms do what needs to be done."

"And sacrifice themselves."

Tanner turned off the highway down a side road and pulled into a little lane that led into someone's field. "Okay, Mom. There's not a soul around but me. Your baby's hungry. I can take a walk if you like."

"Only if you're uncomfortable," she said, blushing again. He thought she looked really pretty when her cheeks pinked up like that. "I mean, I'm going to be doing it at home for a while yet. And I'd rather not hide in the bedroom."

He stared at her. "Hide in the bedroom? Don't be ridiculous. If it's privacy you want, say the word and I'll be the one to leave."

Rowan was still crying. Laura looked as if she

wanted to say something but instead she got out and opened the back door, took Rowan out of the seat and brought her up front. Tanner made sure he focused on whatever was outside his window and not the rustling sounds happening beside him.

"Tanner," she said softly. "It's okay. See?"

He looked over. She'd spread a soft flannel blanket over her shoulder, creating a discreet drape over Rowan's head. But he saw the little feet resting on the curve of Laura's belly, heard the quiet suckling sounds and realized something incredibly new, strange and disconcerting.

The natural act of a woman feeding her child was an intimate and profound thing, filling him with awe and respect and affection and...

He swallowed against a lump in his throat and turned away. And love. There was something so feminine and powerful about it. Rowan must have pulled back and he heard her cough a little bit, and Laura's attention was diverted as she adjusted things. When Tanner glanced over, he caught a glimpse of creamy white breast, and Rowan's soft little head tucked securely against her, obscuring any view of Laura's nipple.

He shifted in his seat and stared, unseeing, out the windshield as minutes ticked by. He was marrying this woman and she was asking him to be her friend. Entertaining thoughts that ran deeper than friendship would only complicate things. But how did you stop thoughts?

"She's asleep, Tanner. I'm going to put her back in her seat and we can be on our way."

He looked over. Laura had adjusted her blouse and it was as if nothing had happened. He pasted on a smile. "No problem. Kid's gotta eat." But when Laura carefully got out to fasten Rowan in her seat, Tanner let out a huge sigh. There was no sense fooling himself. He'd felt something unexpected when he saw the curve of her breast, pictured more. It had been desire, pure and simple. She was a pretty woman, and she was kind and generous, too. A man would be crazy not to fall for that.

He'd have to be careful if they went through with this marriage. She wasn't interested in him that way and he didn't want to make things weird. It was just the stress of the day, he reasoned, and the intimacy of the moment that had gotten to him.

When Laura got back inside the truck, she treated him to a wide smile. "Thank you for stopping," she said. "It'll save me from an embarrassing moment or ten later on."

"No problem," he replied, and put the truck in reverse.

He needed to get them to the ranch. Because if they sat here in the middle of nowhere for much longer, he was going to do something stupid. Like kiss her. And that would throw a monkey wrench into all their plans.

LAURA FOLDED HER hands in her lap, but inside, her stomach was flip-flopping like one of the trout that Gramps used to catch on their Saturday morning fishing trips. It had been totally considerate of Tanner to stop, and a relief, too. But she'd thought he'd hop out of the truck, take a walk. Instead he'd stayed, and she'd tried to be discreet.

Until Rowan had coughed and pulled back, and Laura had had to adjust the baby and blanket. The flannel slipped and for a few moments her breast had been exposed.

It's just a breast, she reminded herself. She was pretty sure Tanner had seen one before. The preposterous idea nearly made her laugh. The difference was he hadn't seen *her* breast before, and he probably hadn't been in a situation where he was on his way to tell his parents he was marrying a woman he didn't love, and on a temporary basis.

And then there was the fact that the idea of him seeing her sent a strange tingling to her core. It wasn't much of a stretch to imagine what it would be like to be loved by a man like Tanner. He was handsome, charming, sexy as hell. Chivalrous and kind. He'd be a gentle lover, she suspected. Gentle and yet intense…

Snap out of it, Laura, she thought, and forced herself to look out the truck window instead of stealing glances at him. Those were her feelings, but they weren't real, she was sure of it. Besides, she was pretty sure there was nothing sexy about watching a woman breast-feed. What had he called it? Oh yes. Practicalities. Not a thing romantic about that, was there?

There was no danger of Tanner having similar feelings, so she might as well push them aside and stop worrying about it.

Her heart rate was nearly back to normal when he finally reached the front gate to the lane leading to the Hudson house. It was probably three times the size of her little bungalow, well-kept and homey looking with balcony planters on the front railing and a pair of wooden rocking chairs out front. A car and a truck already sat in the drive, and she looked over at Tanner, silently questioning.

"My mom's car and my dad's truck," he explained, but she noticed a new tightness to his jaw. This wasn't going to be an easy hour. They were expected for dinner, but as Tanner's obvious nerves proved contagious, Laura wondered if they'd even stay that long.

Might as well get it over with. Cole and Maddy and the boys weren't there at least. Smaller numbers were easier to manage in her limited experience.

"You ready?" she asked, trying to lighten her tone.

"Are you?"

"Tanner, they can't say anything worse than what I've heard whispered around town. But they're your folks. Your relationship with them is important. I'll be fine. It's you I'm worried about."

He reached over and took her hand. "You're a strong woman, you know that?"

"I don't know. I don't think I'm that strong. Maybe I just know what I can't change so I deal with it."

Her fatalistic point of view wasn't as cheering as she'd hoped, but Tanner gave her fingers a final squeeze. "So we're sticking to the seeing-each-other-since-December story?"

She nodded. "I still think it's best."

"Okay. If that's what you want."

She retrieved Rowan from the back and cradled the sleeping baby against her shoulder. Tanner solicitously carried the diaper bag and they walked up to the front door. Laura's insides truly trembled this time. Her grandparents were one thing, but this… this was quite another. She'd probably be judged. Be found lacking. Be asked intrusive questions and she'd be lying, something she was getting used to and didn't like about herself at all.

Tanner must have sensed her anxiety because he'd been about to knock on the door, but instead dropped his hand and turned to face her. His eyes were troubled as he stared down at her, his lips a thin line. "We don't have to do this."

"Meet your parents? Or get married?"

"Either," he confirmed. "I'll help you find another way."

"Why?" she asked, keeping her voice low. Rowan's warm breath made a damp patch on her collar. "Why are you doing this? Why do you even care?"

He lifted his hand and put it gently along her cheek. "Because five months ago I sat in an ambulance with one of the bravest women I'd ever met. That's the only birth I've ever attended, do you know that? Something happened to me that day, and it made me look at things differently. Then when I got to know you better, and you trusted me with the truth… Laura, no one should have to go through that alone. I'd like to think we're friends. And friends help each other."

"This is a pretty big favor. It goes well above and beyond friendship, Tanner."

His charming grin was back. "I don't see anyone else beating down my door looking for happily ever after," he said lightly, chuckling. "This isn't a sacrifice for me, Laura. But somehow I don't think I'll be able to convince you of that."

"I don't deserve this," she murmured, and the hand on her cheek slid down to cup her chin.

"I don't want to hear you say that again, you hear? Everyone deserves a second chance." And he leaned forward and kissed the tip of her nose. Just as the front door opened and Ellen stood in the doorway.

Chapter Eight

Laura stepped back quickly, holding Rowan tight in her arms. Her cheeks flared; she could feel the heat rush into them as Tanner turned to his mother and offered a wide smile. "Hi, Mom."

"Sweetheart," she said, moving forward. "And, Laura. Welcome. Come on in."

Ellen said nothing about the tender moment she'd interrupted, but it had certainly set the tone. Laura could feel Ellen's assessing gaze as they went inside, and Tanner put the diaper bag down on a chair just inside the living room. If he'd wanted to give the impression of romance right off the bat, he'd done a fine job.

"Your dad should be up from the barn any moment," Ellen said. "Would either of you care for a drink or something?"

Tanner looked at her, questioning, and Laura forced a smile. "Maybe some water. That would be great."

"I'll get it," he said, and went to the cupboard for a glass. "Have a seat, Laura. We can sit and relax for a while. Right, Mom?"

"Of course."

And still there was that guarded, questioning look.

"So," Ellen said, her tone deceptively smooth. "You're the one Tanner's been so secretive about."

Laura opened her mouth and closed it again, unsure of how to reply. Tanner handed her a glass of water and smiled. "A man my age doesn't want his mother to know everything," he teased. He looked back at Ellen and sent her an outrageous wink. "We wanted some privacy until we sorted a few things out."

"I see."

Laura doubted that his mom did see, but Tanner was doing a wonderful job of deflecting and she went to his side. They walked into the living room and sat on the sofa while Ellen sank into a plush wing chair. "Thank you for having us over, Mrs. Hudson." This was the woman who, for a short while anyway, would be her mother-in-law. She'd rather have her as an ally than an adversary.

Rowan shifted on her shoulder and Laura made a small adjustment, then saw a softening of Ellen's expression as she looked at the baby. Rowan might just be the ticket here, she realized. From everything Tanner had said, Ellen doted on Maddy's twin boys.

"This is Rowan," Laura said softly, the smile coming naturally as it always did with regards to her daughter. "She's five months old."

"She's beautiful," Ellen acknowledged, a little of the strain leaving her voice. "She's got such a lovely head of dark hair."

Ellen looked up at Laura. Laura's hair, of course, was like waves of copper. Clearly, Rowan didn't get her hair from her mother.

"It was a little lighter when she was first born," Laura offered, touching the soft cap of hair.

"You and Tanner. You're involved?"

"Mom…" Tanner began, but Laura shook her head at him.

"It's okay, Tanner. She's your mom. And while Rowan is still so very tiny, I can imagine that moms always look out for their kids, no matter how old they are." She met Ellen's gaze. "Tanner has been so kind to me ever since the day Rowan was born. He's a rare thing these days, I think. A gentleman through and through." She grinned now, remembering. "He even passed muster with my grandfather, and he's a tough nut to crack."

"You've spent time with Charlie and Patricia?" There was a note of censure in Ellen's tone, as though she was annoyed at being left out.

"Charlie mostly," Tanner said, jumping into the conversation. "He stayed with Laura when Patricia was in the hospital a while back. I ran into Laura and Charlie at the diner one day, and then had dinner with the both of them. He's a real character."

"Always was," Ellen said affectionately. "I'm sorry, Laura. This is just a bit awkward. Considering Maddy and everything. No sense dancing around it."

"I know." Her throat felt tight and her chest small as she faced yet another person's censure. "Maddy and I have made peace, Mrs. Hudson. We talked just before Christmas. Not that we're BFFs or anything, but we're good."

"How can that be?"

Laura pursed her lips. "Honestly, that's between Maddy and me. You'll have to ask her." And Laura hoped if she did she'd keep her secret as she'd promised.

"Laura," Tanner said quietly beside her. She knew

what he wanted. He wanted her to tell the truth. And oh, she was tempted. Just as she had been for months, with the words to vindicate herself sitting on her tongue, ready to be spoken. And then she thought of Spence, and Rowan, and the reason for doing all this in the first place, and she swallowed them down like a bitter pill.

"Mrs. Hudson, there are things you don't know, and things I can't tell you. But if Maddy can forgive me, maybe you can, too?"

The back door opened and shut and Laura realized that Tanner's dad had arrived. The sudden noise of the door stirred Rowan, who nuzzled against Laura's shirt and then lifted her head, rubbing one chubby fist over her nose as she blinked, coming awake. John came in from a back room—Laura assumed it was a back door to a mudroom or some such—and halted at the scene before him. She and Tanner were on one side of the living room, sitting stiffly on the sofa. Ellen was across from them, ensconced in the chair. And they were clearly on different sides of the conversation.

"Hope I'm not too late," he said cautiously.

"Of course not, Dad." Tanner stood and stepped forward to shake his father's hand, causing a look of confusion to pass over John's face. "Have you met Laura?"

"Mr. Hudson," she said, smiling and offering a small nod. She held Rowan with her right arm, which made shaking hands cumbersome, so she decided a smile would have to do.

"Hello," he said, then looked at Tanner, glanced at his wife, and back to Laura again. "Who have we here?"

"This is my daughter, Rowan. Tanner helped deliver her last December."

It was easy to tell when John understood. His eyes widened slightly and his gaze darted to Tanner again. "Oh," he said, and that was all for a few moments. Then his eyebrows lifted again and he peered at her shoulder. "She's a sweet one." He smiled and his whole face softened. John Hudson liked babies. That might work in their favor, too.

"Yes, she is. Sleeping through the night most of the time, which is a great relief to me." Laura felt herself relax just a little. Tanner's father felt like an ally. Mothers were bound to be the overprotective ones, weren't they? Particularly with their sons?

There was a momentary distraction as Ellen asked John about a cup of coffee and gave him a phone message, so Laura turned to Tanner and let out a breath.

"Your mom isn't happy."

"She'll come around."

"But we haven't even mentioned the wedding yet." That troubled her. And she'd brought Maddy into it without intending to. "Right now she just thinks we're dating." Laura bit down on her lip.

She needed to compose herself if they were going to get through this visit. "Could you show me where the bathroom is? I need to excuse myself for a moment."

"Of course."

Tanner led her down a short hall, but once there he reached for Rowan. "Let me take her for a few minutes."

"Are you sure?" She realized he hadn't held her much, except for that brief time at the café when she'd turned her back and changed her shirt.

"Of course I'm sure. I've held her before. And it's only for a few minutes."

She eased Rowan into his arms, seeing his biceps curl in his shirt sleeve as he bent his arm to cradle her close.

She sighed, getting a swirly, silly feeling at seeing her baby daughter in his strong arms. What was it about tough men and babies and puppies that turned women into mush anyway?

She turned around and resolutely went into the bathroom and shut the door behind her.

When she returned to the living room, Tanner sat on one end of the sofa, with Rowan sitting on his thigh and leaning back against the wall of his chest, patting her hands together happily. His parents were seated in matching chairs across from him, smiling at Rowan and something Tanner was saying.

He looked up when she approached. "Hey. I was just telling Mom and Dad about you and your battery and then Ro had a big burp. Cracked us up." He grinned at her, as if her daughter's gas was the most amusing thing in the world. God, he could be sweet.

"Classy," she replied, trying to keep the mood light for as long as they could. She sat down beside him, not too close, but close enough. Rowan seemed content, so Laura left her where she was. It was strange, knowing she and Tanner weren't an actual couple, and yet feeling a certain intimacy with him that suggested they were.

"So you've been seeing each other awhile now, I take it?" This came from John.

Tanner met Laura's gaze. His eyes were warm on hers—he was a better actor than she expected. Then he took her hand. "For a while," he agreed, looking back at his parents. "We came over today to tell you we're getting married."

The warm vibe shattered as Ellen's mouth fell open and John's mouth pursed and a furrow appeared on his brow.

"Married?" There was no way to describe his mother's tone other than shocked and dismayed.

He nodded, the same relaxed smile on his face, but his fingers had tightened over hers.

"Yes, married." He faced them squarely. "Considering the circumstances, we're going to have a small civil ceremony and I'll be moving into her place."

"Circumstances? You're not… I mean, Rowan's so small."

It took a few moments for Laura to comprehend what Ellen was asking, and as soon as she understood, heat rushed to her face. "Oh, gosh no! I'm not pregnant, if that's what you mean." She was so flustered she said the only thing that popped into her head. "Goodness, I just started getting a full night's sleep."

Tanner chuckled, down low. She closed her eyes momentarily, completely embarrassed. She'd made it sound as if she was too tired for sex. Which she usually was, although when Tanner looked at her a certain way she didn't suppose she'd be too hard to convince. And it wasn't that she actually wanted his parents to think they were sleeping together. She couldn't think of a graceful out to save herself.

Not for the first time since arriving, she wished she could become invisible.

It was a blessed relief when Ellen shifted the subject slightly. "But, Tanner, I thought you were apartment-hunting."

Laura hadn't expected a warm reception to their news, but somehow Ellen's response made her feel small and unwanted. Her fingers tightened on Tanner's, too, like holding on to a lifeline. They didn't have to do this—he'd said so. And here he was, facing his parents head-on. She felt like she should be the one to give him the out—only he'd been the one to do the asking in the first place. What a jumble.

"I was, but then I realized it was stupid to sign a lease, when…" He looked at Laura. She couldn't help the moisture that gathered in her eyes at his warm expression. What had she done to deserve such a champion? When Tanner smiled reassuringly, she gathered strength and faced his parents.

"Mr. and Mrs. Hudson, I know this is a surprise. And I know I'm probably your last choice for a daughter-in-law. I also know what people say about me here in Gibson."

"Laura," Tanner said in a low voice, but she shook her head.

"It's okay, Tanner. People think Rowan is Gavin Wallace's baby. I know that. I've always known that."

"Are you saying she's not? If Gavin's not the father, who is?" Ellen leaned forward, her gaze intent on Laura.

Laura hesitated, and then looked at Ellen evenly. "Frankly, it's nobody's business."

"Tanner?" Ellen stared at him next. "Are you saying you don't know and you don't care?"

"I do know," he said quietly. "And it doesn't matter to me, truly. It's Laura's business, and hers to share if she wishes. She's shared the truth with me, and I respect her for that."

Laura peered at Tanner's father. Mercy, the two of them looked alike. Thick dark hair, though the elder Hudson's was sprinkled with gray. Deep blue eyes, strong jaw. Tanner's expressions were more roguish than his dad's, but now, when the discussion was serious, she could see so much of his father in him. John Hudson was the kind of man who, when he spoke, people listened. Not so much with Tanner, and she wondered if that was behind his need to break away and do his own thing. He was the younger son and Cole was popular in Gibson. Maybe Tanner was tired of always being in the shadows and wanted to get out and be his own man.

"Are you ready to be a father, son? Because when you marry a woman with a child, that's what you are. A father. In all but blood."

Laura held her breath. They hadn't really talked about his role with Rowan.

"Yes, sir," he replied, still holding her child close in his arms. Rowan's little fingers wrapped around his index one. "I'm going to be there, for Laura and for Rowan, and whatever they need."

Oh God, she wasn't sure she could do this. It was all such a big lie. And Tanner was making it sound like undeniable, unimpeachable truth. Guilt and fear crowded in on her. How had she ever agreed to go through with this? So much could go wrong!

Remorse stuck in her throat and she swallowed around the lump of it. Maybe she should just come clean. But then she looked at Tanner and couldn't say anything. The words wouldn't come. The truth of it hit her then. Deep down, she wanted this. Even if he never felt anything romantic for her, even if they ended up divorcing after a year or two, she wanted this now. She wanted him not for his protection, but for his companionship. She wanted to feel she wasn't so alone in the world, as though she mattered to someone, as though someone mattered to her. Oh sure, there was Rowan, and having her had made her experience a love far deeper than she'd ever known. But this was different.

She wanted a kind of fairy tale—even if it was all pretend. For however long, there'd be someone there with her at the end of the day, across the table, someone to share a morning coffee with or laugh at a movie or TV show.

It wasn't as if there was a lineup of candidates anxious to fill the position. Tanner would also give her the protection of his name. Ironically, it was binding herself in marriage that would free her.

She looked first at his father, then his mother, and this time there was no hesitation in her voice when she spoke.

"Tanner is the kindest, gentlest, most generous person I've ever known. I'm aware that the honor of this is entirely mine, and I'm crazy lucky that he asked me to marry him. I'll try every day to make sure he doesn't regret it. He's a good man and he's…he's my best friend."

Tanner was looking at her now with something like admiration and surprise. "Best friends, huh?" he asked, and her heart gave a solid whump at the tender look in his eyes.

She knew how pathetic it probably sounded. She didn't really have friends here. The few she'd met with after she'd moved home quickly distanced themselves from her when the rumors started.

She nodded a little, and stared down at her lap. And was surprised when he scooched over and slid his free arm around her, so they made a unit: her, Tanner and Rowan, who had turned on his lap and now played with one of the buttons on his shirt.

Ellen's expression had softened, but Laura still sensed a certain amount of reserve. "Tanner, what about Maddy? You know she and Cole are probably going to announce their engagement any time. I don't mean to be crass, Laura, but it could make for some tense situations in the family."

This one Laura could field with a little confidence. "As I said, we've made our peace. Cole, too. We'll probably never be close friends, but we have an understanding. That's not to say it won't be awkward, I guess. Which is another reason to keep the wedding small."

"You don't want a regular wedding? In a church with the dress and flowers and so on?"

Oh, she had wanted that, once upon a time. But her choices had led her to this moment, and a big wedding would be highly inappropriate. Even if it had been the real McCoy, based on love and everything...making a wedding a big production would be tactless given the situation, and a bigger expense than either of them could justify.

"I'd like something small. Just the two of us..." She looked at Rowan and corrected herself. "...the three of us, and a few witnesses, and maybe a few little flowers. A bride should have flowers."

The words came out and it was all she could do to

keep her emotions in check. She wouldn't cry. Not here, not in front of Tanner's parents...not ever.

Quiet fell over the room for several long moments. Finally, Ellen sighed. "I don't mean to be a Negative Nelly. It's just a shock. We didn't even know you were involved. And now marriage... What's the rush? Surely, you can wait. Plan a proper wedding, say six months from now or so. It just seems so fast."

How could Laura possibly explain the necessity for expediency? In six months Spence would be eligible to apply for parole. Not to mention her employment situation. While she fumbled with words, Tanner once again stepped in.

"Because this is what we want, Mom. We've talked it over."

"But, Tanner—"

"Ellen, leave the boy alone," his father said firmly. "He's a grown man, able to make his own decisions and learn from his own mistakes."

Laura's already low spirits plummeted. That was all she was—a mistake. A bad decision. It could be the sweetness from the cinnamon buns at her grandparents' or the coffee she hadn't had for months, but she doubted that was behind the sick feeling in the pit of her stomach.

"Maybe we should go," she suggested on a whisper, avoiding Tanner's gaze. "And give them a chance to get used to the news."

"That's probably a good idea," Tanner agreed, and the smile he'd kept on his face for the last hour had faded. "Plus, Rowan didn't have much of a nap." The baby was rubbing a fist against her eyes, a sure sign she was tired and ready for sleep. Laura knew Rowan could sleep like an angel in her arms, but it was as good an excuse to leave as any.

"You're not staying for dinner?"

"I don't think so, Mom. Thanks anyway. We'd better get Rowan home."

It only took a few seconds for them to gather their things, but it was long enough for Laura to understand that Tanner had made a stand today. He'd stood for her and for her daughter. It still befuzzled her why he'd do that, but he had his reasons.

"Tanner, are you... Will you be home tonight?" They'd stopped at the door, preparing to say their goodbyes, when Ellen's hesitant question halted them.

"Yes, I'll be home," he said, patting her shoulder. "Besides, I want to talk to Cole."

"Of course you do."

They didn't say anything to Laura. She tried not to be hurt by it, but she was just the same. After months of suffering sidelong looks and whispers, she thought she'd have a tougher skin by now. Not so, it seemed. She'd felt small and, well, a bit like someone's dirty laundry. Worst of all, she'd wanted it to go well for Tanner's sake. Now he was caught in the middle.

He didn't say anything the whole way back to her place. But when they arrived, he hopped out of the truck and rushed around to open her door for her, then reached in for the car seat and carried Rowan to the front door.

Once inside, Laura released the breath she'd been holding. This was her house. It wasn't much, but it was hers, and it was a little oasis where she didn't feel she had to prove anything. It was such a relief to be under her own roof again.

Tanner shut the door, put down the car seat with a slumbering Rowan inside and placed his hands on Laura's shoulders.

"Are you okay?" he asked.

Despite her earlier determination, she took one look at him and started to cry.

Chapter Nine

Tanner was not used to dealing with crying women.

He made it a policy to keep things light and non-committal. A few dates and he moved on before any serious attachments could be made. But this was different. For one thing, he and Laura weren't in love. And for another, she was about to become his wife and she'd called him her best friend.

It had been a hard afternoon and she'd borne the brunt of it. So he gathered her against his chest, put his arms around her and let her cry it out.

"I'm sorry," she wailed softly after a few minutes of gulping and sobbing. "I don't usually cry. I just…" She stopped midsentence and sniffed again.

"You just what?" he asked gently, stroking her back with his hand.

After a few moments, he heard the words muffled against his shirt. "I felt so small. So…dirty."

"Oh, honey." His heart went out to her. Letting everyone think Gavin was the father of her baby had cost her plenty. Telling them the truth wouldn't help, either—this was a small town where a baby fathered by a felon was pretty much on par with an extramarital affair.

"I should never have come back here. I should have gone to a city somewhere. Gotten lost in the crowds, been anonymous."

"Except you wanted to come home," he supplied, still rubbing her back.

She nodded and snuffled. "I did. I needed somewhere familiar. I needed what little family I have. I know I'm undesirable. *I know it.* But it still hurts when it's pointed out."

He was treading on treacherous ground. How much did he want to tell her about his feelings? About how he felt this unexplainable need to make sure that Rowan—and Laura—were cared for? Getting to know her better only proved he was right. She was a kind, sweet person who was scared and misunderstood.

"You're not undesirable," he said gently, pressing his lips against her hair. "I promise you, Laura. People see the mistakes, but they don't see the wonderful things about you. Human nature is always that way, though it shouldn't be."

"Look at me," she contradicted. "I'm a single mom who…well, I'm living in fear, aren't I?" She pushed against his chest and peered up at him, and his heart ached at the sight of her red eyes and tear-streaked cheeks. "I've made so many mistakes, and now all I know how to do is run. Do you know how much I hate that about myself? That instead of standing up and fighting, I'm making decisions on how to hide better?"

He raised his hand and ran his thumb over her cheek. "You're a mom. Moms do what they need to do to protect their children. No one can blame you for being mama bear."

She shook her head. "Tanner, you're wasting your

time with me. Why tie yourself down for a year or two when you could be out looking for Miss Right? Someone far more suitable than me? Someone your family will approve of and welcome with open arms?" To his dismay, her tears welled again and she dropped her chin. "Someone worthy of the kind of man you are."

"I don't ever want to hear you say that again." Tanner's heart pounded painfully, hating how negative she was about herself. "You are not unworthy. You are definitely not undesirable, Laura. If you could see you the way I see you…"

She bit down on her lip.

He sighed, lifted her chin with his finger. "You are a tigress. I watched you bring that sweet baby girl into the world with a ferocity that was mind-blowing. You have endured the looks and the gossip for months in order to protect yourself and your baby, even though it cost you a lot personally. You are one of the strongest women I've ever met, and if people can't see that, then that's their problem."

He knew he shouldn't, but he ran his hand through her hair, the thick coppery strands slipping over his fingers like silk. She had a few pale freckles on her cheeks, just on either side of her nose, and they made her look young and artless. Her bottom lip was swollen and plump from where she'd bitten down on it. She was so damn beautiful.

"Tanner?" she whispered, her voice unsure. And it was that question that moved him forward, so close that their bodies brushed as his hand cradled her head and he kissed her.

He meant for it to be a kiss of reassurance, something gentle and affirming, to let her know that she was, indeed, desirable. He failed utterly, because the moment his mouth was on hers, there was nothing gentle or reassuring about it. Her breath caught deliciously as her lips opened beneath his, as instinctive as a flower turning toward the sun. His body felt super-charged and he pulled her closer, losing himself in the sweet taste of her. When she made a little sound in her throat, he nearly lost his mind. He threaded his other hand through her hair and tilted her head back, sliding his lips from hers and trailing them down the soft skin of her neck.

She cried out, a thin impassioned sound that only fired him up further. When her hips rubbed against his, he ground back, loving the feel of her. She fit against him just right, and he licked a path from the hollow of her throat up to her earlobe, and she spread her hands on his back, holding him close.

He disentangled one hand and slid it down to cup her full breast. The tip was hard and pebbled against his hand, but that was when Laura suddenly backed off, pressing her fingers on his wrist, pushing him away. He let her; he wasn't into coercion or force. Instead he listened to their breathing echoing through the kitchen, marveling that a few minutes ago she'd been crying against him and now his brain was a complete fog, filled with the haze of wanting her.

"Oh God," she said, leaning back against the wall and resting her head against the firm surface. "That was...oh, dammit."

"Dammit? Was it that bad?" He tried a little joke, anything to lighten the tension. She wanted to stop. He needed to stop thinking what it would be like to carry her into her bedroom and finish this properly.

"We can't… We shouldn't… This would complicate everything." Her wary eyes watched him, but he
could only see her lips, so obviously freshly kissed.

"We have an agreement," she reminded him. "Platonic. In name only. Tanner, if we do this—get married, I mean—you can't be kissing me in the kitchen."

He didn't realize that he'd rubbed his hand over his
zipper until he saw her eyes widen and her cheeks turn
hot pink. "Can I kiss you in the living room, then? In
your bedroom?" He smiled at her, teasing, but deep
down he was just as confused as she was. That wasn't
supposed to happen. Not that fast. Not that hot and
demanding.

"Be serious," she said. And then she looked down
at herself and cursed softly, not quite under her breath.

It took a moment, but he saw what caused her con-
sternation when he dropped his gaze to her chest.

"Sexy, isn't it?" At least it was a distraction and a
good "deflating" change of topic. "Gotta love oxy-
tocin."

Tanner was a rancher. He knew enough about ani-
mals to know what happened when females nursed.
What he hadn't realized was that arousal caused the
same chemical reaction. He wasn't sure if he was hor-
rified or terribly intrigued.

"It's probably for the best," she continued, sliding
away from him and rolling her shoulders. "We needed
to stop."

He wasn't so sure of that, but he could tell she was,
and that was all that mattered. "I didn't expect it to be
so…well. Explosive."

She was a good five, six feet away now, a safe distance. It didn't feel very safe, though, when she looked

up and met his gaze. The fire was still there, just waiting for a puff of oxygen to fan the flames. "I guess it's been a big dry spell for me," she countered.

For him, too. Longer than most people would believe, given his reputation. But that wasn't it. Dry spells were mere convenient excuses. It was probably better to agree with her, though, than to point out that they had incendiary chemistry.

"Now do you believe you're desirable?" he asked, taking a small step backward and trying hard to relax his tense muscles.

"Is that what that was? Trying to prove a point?"

He swallowed against the lump in his throat. "At first. You were so sad and pretty and I wanted to kiss you and make you feel better, but as soon as I did…"

There she was, biting on that lip again. He really wished she wouldn't. It was sexy as hell.

"It got away from us," she said.

"It sure did."

She turned away and he smiled a little as she tossed her hair over her shoulder. She had spunk and she didn't even realize it.

"Getting married is probably a mistake," she said.

"You've changed your mind?" He knew she was simply reacting to what had happened. It had thrown them both.

She shrugged. He saw her inhale, then exhale slowly before turning around. "I don't know. This complicates things a lot."

"It doesn't have to happen again," he assured her. He could control himself, after all.

"It doesn't have to, but it doesn't mean it won't."

Tanner went to her then. He saw her eyes widen at

his approach, wondering if he was going to kiss her again. But he didn't. He put his hands lightly on her shoulders and looked down at her. "Nothing will happen that you don't want," he said firmly. "I'm not into persuasion or forcing my hand."

Laura gazed up at him for so long he thought he might drown in them. "You mean that," she whispered.

"You have my word." As much as he hated to give it, he would. Because it was what she needed right now.

"Maybe…" She started to speak and then stopped, frowning. "Hmm."

"Maybe what?"

"Maybe what we need to do is give this a trial run. You know, before the ceremony. It's three weeks away. You could move your stuff in here in the meantime and we could see how we get along. If it doesn't work, we cancel the wedding and that's it. I figure out something else and you can resume your apartment-hunting. We'd only be out the marriage license and the fee for the officiant."

He considered for a moment. It was actually a very practical, very sound plan.

"Then tomorrow we have some things to do, don't we?"

"We do?"

He nodded. "We're supposed to go for the marriage license. Then we'll shop for a bed afterward, and I'll bring what I need over tomorrow night after work and dinner."

"You're sure?"

He nodded. "I think it's a smart idea. It gives us a chance to get used to each other. Settle in. Besides, then we won't be worried about it for the next three weeks. We'll have all that adjustment stuff down pat."

It sounded great, except for just one thing. While he could promise he wouldn't touch her or make any moves, he couldn't promise not to think about it. He knew from experience that thinking too much could just about do a man in.

"And no more funny business." She pointed a finger at him and then dropped it, giving a small, slightly crooked smile. "Isn't that what you said that first night?"

It was, and he found it telling that she remembered. Had it been on her mind?

"Laura, I find you incredibly attractive and I like you a lot. But I made a promise. So if anything happens between us, it'll be because you come to me. Okay?"

She gave a tiny nod. "Okay. So no worries there, then."

"No worries there."

It was only one kiss. They'd get over it.

"Now, are you okay? I should get back home. I told Mom I would. Plus I need to break the news that I'm moving out *and* talk to Cole."

"Sounds like a fun evening."

"It could be a lot worse." He laughed a little. In fact, despite tonight's confusing events, he was looking forward to it. A guy could only live with his parents for so long before wanting to get out on his own. Even if the arrangement was slightly unorthodox. "I'll see you tomorrow, then? I'll come by and pick you up late morning, is that okay? We'll get the license thing looked after and whatever else needs doing."

"Okay," she answered, smiling back.

There was a moment before he left that they both hesitated and the kitchen was quiet. It was a moment in which a regular couple would come together for a goodbye kiss, or a hug, or their hands would twine together and then drift apart—or all three. Instead Tanner stepped forward and kissed the crest of her cheek, keeping his hands to himself. "See you in the morning. Get a good night's sleep."

It wasn't until he was seated in his truck with the engine running that he completely relaxed his shoulders and allowed his real thoughts permission to run freely.

The truth was he was starting to really care for Laura, far beyond friendship or responsibility or to serve his own purposes. He'd explained those feelings away for weeks now, but he couldn't explain away the reaction he had to her kisses or the feel of her body against his.

That kind of passion didn't happen every day. And when it did happen, and with someone he also liked and wanted to care for...

This marriage wasn't going to be as platonic as he had thought. At least not for him. For his own sake, they'd best keep it short, then.

LAURA GATHERED THE sheets from the dryer and took them into the bedroom, making up the bed fresh. Tonight Tanner would be sleeping in it. It would be his long body beneath the covers; his head on the pillow.

The day had passed in a blur. First, they'd gone to the county office for their marriage license, which had been nothing more than official paperwork and certainly nothing romantic about it. They'd gone from there to a furniture store in Great Falls—one of those discount chain places—and Tanner had bought her a single bed, complete with mattress. Laura hadn't liked that too much, but she didn't have the cash pay for such a purchase. And then Tanner pointed out he was taking her bed, and if he moved into an apartment he'd have to buy furniture anyway and also pay first and last month's rent. When he put it that way, she didn't feel quite so bad. When they stopped at the department store in Gibson, she made sure she paid for the new sheets, comforter, and extra pillow.

It was as if the previous evening hadn't happened. Nothing improper, no long, lingering looks or touches. Nothing to suggest that less than twenty-four hours earlier she'd been twined around him like a vine on a fence post, clinging to his lips like a blossom reaching for the sun.

When they'd finally arrived home again, she helped him carry in the heavy boxes containing the bed parts. He'd be over later to put it together, bringing his things with him. All very practical and businesslike.

In the meantime, she'd put Rowan down for a nap and was working on making her room into Tanner's. This job seemed far more personal, because she was making room for him in her house. In her life.

She sorted through Rowan's things and packed away anything she'd outgrown, and then took the bottom two dresser drawers for herself. The rest of her clothes she stored in Rowan's small closet, hanging up what she could and putting some on the top shelf. Her "good" clothes she left in her bedroom closet, pushed over to one side to make room for Tanner's.

The computer she left where it was, at least for now. During the day, Tanner would be at the ranch, so she could come in here and work. If it became a problem, they could look at moving her desk somewhere else, though the living room was pretty small for more furniture.

Rowan woke and Laura fed her. Lately, Ro had been fussing more and more, and Laura figured it was probably past time to start feeding her some solids. Particularly since she'd started waking in the night again. After taking forty-five minutes to change and feed her, she put Rowan on a blanket in the living room and threw the new bedding in the washing machine. She heated up a can of soup and made a peanut butter sandwich to go with it, and by the time Tanner arrived at seven, she had Rowan in the bathtub, splashing happily.

"Hello?" he called, and Laura's stomach filled with butterflies. *He's here.*

"We're in the bathroom," she called. Even though the baby was in a type of ring that kept her from sliding in the tub, Laura wouldn't leave her alone. She soaped up the washcloth, preparing to cut bath playtime short since Tanner had already arrived.

He peeked into the bathroom and leaned on the door frame. "Well. Someone likes her bath."

Rowan splashed with both hands, slapping the water and giggling at the sound and the droplets that were flung in and out of the tub.

"Always," Laura agreed. "I'll be a few minutes here. I made room for your things in the bedroom and put fresh bedding on the bed. You can bring your stuff in if you want."

"Sounds good."

She was dying to know how it had all gone at his parents' place. If they weren't thrilled about the wedding, they probably had their noses out of joint about him moving in with her so quickly.

While she finished with Rowan, she heard him making trips back and forth from his truck to the bedroom. When Rowan was finally snapped into her pajamas, Laura hung up the towel and put the baby on her shoulder, then went out to investigate.

Tanner didn't have suitcases. Instead, two large duffel bags sat on the floor in her room, as well as a couple of cardboard boxes. "That's it?" she asked. "It sounded like you made more trips than that."

"I did. I brought some tools and stuff and put them in the basement. I figure it wouldn't hurt for me to take on some odd jobs around here, right?"

She rubbed Rowan's back absently. "Odd jobs?"

He nodded, wiping his hands on his jeans. "You know, like maybe painting the front railing and trim. I noticed one of the steps could use replacing, too, and the soffit needs tending." He grinned at her. "Might as well earn my keep."

She wasn't sure what to say. It would be nice to have those things done, but it wasn't because she couldn't do them. Deciding it would be best to simply be honest, she met his gaze squarely. "Tanner, I can paint and even fix the step. The reason I haven't is that I prioritized my spending and fresh paint was more of a want than a need."

"I figured that. But it's June and I bet you've paid your mortgage for the month already, haven't you?"

"Yes."

"Then I'll pick up some supplies and putter away in the evenings in lieu of rent for this month."

"But you bought the bed. That was instead of first and last month's…"

"And you have all the rest of the furniture. Trust me, Laura, I'm the one getting a bargain here. Besides, maybe you can help me."

His smile was so big that she couldn't argue with him. It would be nice to spruce up the place a bit. Hadn't she been lamenting the fact not long ago?

Through it all, Rowan was just looked around, wide-eyed. Tanner laughed. "Wow. I'm not sure the kid approves. Look at that face." Indeed, Rowan seemed very sober.

"She's getting tired," Laura said. "I was thinking, maybe we can put off putting the bed together until tomorrow. I'll just sleep on the mattress tonight."

"You're sure?"

She nodded. "By the time we unpack the pieces and get them put together, she'll be beyond ready for bed. I've got the bedding. We can flop down the mattress. It'll be just as comfortable."

They were still standing in between the living room and kitchen. Belatedly, Laura stepped back. "You'd probably like to unpack, though. What time do you get up in the morning?"

He stuck his hands in his pockets. "I should be out the door by seven or so. I'll try not to wake you both."

"Okay. There's bread and jam for toast, or cereal for your breakfast. And eggs in the fridge. Just help yourself. This is your place now, too." It felt so weird to say it. This wasn't just her place anymore. It was theirs. And would be theirs until they decided otherwise.

"Sounds fine. I'll go put my stuff away, I guess."

"The chest of drawers is empty," she said, calling after him as he walked down the hall.

For a good half hour, she heard sounds coming from the bedroom; drawers opened and shut and the odd zipper rasped through the silence. Rowan started fussing and it was close to bedtime, so while Tanner finished up, Laura settled back in the corner of the sofa and nursed. For the first time in months, she longed for a glass of wine to steady her nerves. It was weird. So real, now that he was here in the house, larger than life and with his sunny smile. She'd just tucked everything back into place when Tanner came out, his hair mussed as if he'd run his hands through it several times.

"There. I think I'm mostly set. I feel like a heel, kicking you out of your room, though."

They were going to be married. If they were like a normal married couple, no one would be kicked out of anywhere because they would be sharing a room. But not here, no, sir.

"Don't think anything of it. I'll be snug as a bug in there." She smiled. "Besides, the new bed is far more comfortable than the blow-up mattress."

He perched on the edge of a chair, looked at Rowan's sleeping face for a moment, and then back at her. "This feels weird, doesn't it?"

She let out a relieved breath. "A little. We'll adjust. It's a crazy thing we're doing, after all."

"Yep." He slapped his knee lightly with his hand. "I brought a six-pack over and I feel like a beer. Do you mind?"

"Of course not."

"You want one?"

She glanced at Rowan. "I probably shouldn't."

"Okay." He got up and went to the kitchen. She heard him open the beer and a minute later he was back. He carried a small glass with him, a scant few inches of beer in it. He handed it to her with a wink.

"Maybe just a bit to toast?" he asked.

He was too cute to resist when he looked at her that way, all devilment and sexiness and with his silly hair sticking up on one side. She took the glass and grinned. "Oh, what the heck?" she said.

He lifted his bottle. "To you and Rowan and me. New beginnings, unorthodox arrangements and a bright future ahead for all of us."

Laura lifted her glass and swallowed it all in one gulp, the creamy, fizzy beer sliding down her throat easily. She handed it back to him. "That was quite a speech."

He poured a little more in the glass and handed it back. "It's true, though. We might not be doing things the normal way, but it's for all the right reasons, don't you think?"

This time she didn't answer, but she drank the sip he'd added to her glass. All the right reasons? In her whole life, she'd never considered marrying for anything but love. And that was conspicuously absent.

The thought made her more than a little sad.

Chapter Ten

Laura slept fitfully that night. It wasn't the bed or being in the same room as Rowan; she'd done that when her grandfather came to stay and was used to it. It was knowing Tanner was down the hall, sleeping in her old room. It was remembering the banal, ordinary sounds of another person in the house getting ready for bed. A door shutting, the tap running as he brushed his teeth, the gentle creak of the mattress as he got into bed.

Tonight he'd acted as if their kiss had never happened. As if he'd never licked the sensitive skin of her neck or run his hand over her breast. She swallowed in the darkness, staring at the ceiling. She didn't want a real marriage. She didn't want to care for him or feel this inconvenient attraction, but she couldn't always control it. She remembered something her grandma had told her when she was a teenager and everything with friends and boys seemed so dramatic. "Nothin' you can do about other people, sweetie," she'd said. "The only thing you can control is how you react. You're in charge."

She was in charge. So while she might get a fluttery feeling when Tanner walked into a room, while she already liked the way the house felt with someone else in it, she was still in charge of her actions. Tanner need never know any of how she was feeling. As far as he was concerned, they would strictly be roommates.

She finally drifted off to sleep, only to be wakened early by the sound of Tanner rising and getting ready to leave for work. She stayed curled under her blankets, waiting for him to leave for the day. Rowan slept on, the soft sound of her deep breathing barely audible in the room. Laura checked her watch. It was only six-thirty. When Tanner closed the front door behind him ten minutes later, she let out a deep sigh and went back to sleep.

Her day progressed fairly normally after that. There was laundry, tidying, and caring for Rowan. Now that plans were in place, she booted up her computer and tried to ignore the signs that Tanner now occupied the bedroom, focusing instead on sending out emails to former clients to try to drum up business, then working on her own website design now that she had a launch date of right after the wedding. She threw together a quick sandwich for lunch and had just changed Rowan's wet diaper when she heard a car pull into the driveway.

When she looked out, her heart did an awkward skip. It was Maddy, the last person she'd expected.

Maddy. Gavin's widow. And probably soon to be Tanner's sister-in-law—and hers, as well. Maddy, who up until Christmas thought that Rowan was her husband's daughter. To say things were awkward between them was an understatement. What on earth did she want? It had to be something to do with Tanner. Laura twisted her fingers together. Damn.

It didn't help that Maddy was so pretty. Laura had dated Gavin once upon a time, sure, but the woman he'd married made Laura feel hokey and, well, inadequate. Maddy wasn't just beautiful. She was a kind, generous human being, a wonderful mother, the town sweetheart who could do no wrong. It wasn't a competition by any means, but Laura felt that she fell shy of the mark when standing next to Maddy.

Maddy knocked on the door. Laura counted to three, and then opened it, putting on a polite smile at the same time.

"Maddy. This is a surprise." She injected as much warmth as she could into the words. She didn't dislike Maddy at all; she was simply nervous.

"Hi, Laura. May I come in?"

"Please do." She stood aside and opened the door wider. "Can I get you anything? Something to drink?"

"No, thanks." Maddy smiled at her and Laura felt marginally better. Nothing about the woman sent an adversarial message. "I was wondering if we could talk for a few minutes."

"Of course." Laura led the way through to the living room. "Do you mind if we sit in here? I've got Rowan in her Exersaucer. It keeps her occupied. She likes spinning around." True enough, when they entered the room Rowan gave a little bounce with her feet as she sat in the middle of the contraption, and then spun a quarter turn to bat at a bar holding a colorful wheel.

Maddy grinned. "Oh, we had those for the boys. Gosh, they loved them. When they got older, they jumped so much we thought they would bounce themselves right across the floor." She laughed. "Now I wish I could stick them in it again. They're mobile and holy terrors."

It seemed motherhood was a great shared topic. It also helped that Maddy was one of the few who knew that Rowan wasn't Gavin's child.

"So," Laura said, as they sat.

"I'm here about Tanner. But you probably knew that already." Maddy's lips were slightly pursed, a small frown marring her perfect eyebrows.

"I didn't, but thanks for getting right to the point." Laura folded her hands and regarded Maddy evenly. "I didn't have a chance to speak to Tanner about what happened with you and Cole. He brought his stuff over last night and was gone early this morning, before we got up."

"He didn't waste any time moving out."

Laura hesitated, not wanting to rush her words. "I guess you guys don't approve, huh."

"It's so fast." Maddy's eyes searched hers. "Laura, I'm not trying to judge you. But I do find it hard to believe that you and Tanner are ready for marriage. You can't have been seeing each other very long."

"How long were you with Cole when you knew?" Laura asked the question, knowing fully it was a deliberate diversion, and that it was playing into the lie that this was a love match.

Maddy's cheeks turned pink and she smiled softly. "Not long. A month? But we're not rushing to the altar, either."

Laura shrugged. "That's between you and Cole, Maddy. Tanner asked me, and I said yes. It's only a few weeks until the wedding, so he decided he might as well move in now. It's no big deal."

"No big deal?" Maddy's voice rose and she stood for a moment, turning away briefly before turning back again. "Laura. Please. I know how hard it is to be a single mom. I know what you told me about Rowan's father, too. Tanner told us that you've told him everything. Have you?"

Unease settled heavily in Laura's stomach. "More than I've told either of you," she admitted. "I wouldn't go into this hiding things from him."

Maddy's shoulders relaxed a little. "I'm glad. He deserves honesty."

"You're protecting him, and I get that. But he's a big boy. He knows his own mind. You don't understand. He's kind and gentle and funny and easy to be around and…" She ran out of descriptors but was shocked to see a warmth in Maddy's eyes now.

"You really do love him."

The words seemed to suck all the wind out of her sails. Laura was speechless for a second, knowing Maddy was wrong, but unable to protest without giving herself away, knowing if she did it wouldn't be completely truthful. She did like Tanner. In love with him? No. But neither was she completely immune. Maybe he could pretend their searing kiss hadn't happened, but she couldn't. She didn't want to.

It had been nothing short of splendid.

"Maddy, I'm not exactly comfortable talking about this with you," she said, hoping to dodge the bullet. "Because of the circumstances and because we're not exactly friends. Not that I dislike you in any way. Please don't think that!" she hastened to add. "It's just that I don't have many friends left here in Gibson, and I'm not used to talking about my personal life."

Maddy laughed. "Good Lord. Ask me how many friends I've lost since Gavin died. When the gossip started, it was like I'd somehow changed. People gave me their sympathy but kept their distance. I don't talk about my personal life, either."

Guilt bore its weight on Laura. "God. I hadn't considered that. Oh, Maddy, I'm sorry. That's my fault. I should have made it clear from the start... I just didn't know what to do."

"It's water under the bridge," Maddy assured her. "I'm happy now, and that's the main thing. But I don't want to see you and Tanner leap into anything that's not going to make you both happy. Cole told me to leave it alone, but..." She shrugged helplessly. "Tanner's a great guy. And despite the situation, you haven't exactly got it easy in this town. I don't want either one of you to get hurt."

It was a magnanimous gesture, and knowing Maddy's reputation as she did, Laura had no doubt it was sincere. There wasn't a false bone in her body. It was a little intimidating being faced with all that perfection.

Laura looked at Maddy, trying to envision a world where the two of them might be friends. If it weren't for the history, it would be easy. Maddy was extremely likable. Perhaps a little too perfect, but she didn't throw it in anyone's face or act superior. "Maddy," she asked cautiously, "is Tanner's family really that upset?"

"Bah, bah, bah!" babbled Rowan, an abrupt sound in the stillness as Maddy considered her answer.

"Upset? I don't know about that. Concerned? Sure. Have you really been seeing each other since Christmas?"

"He helped deliver Rowan." She had to expect these sorts of questions and how to answer them. "It's a pretty intimate experience, you know. And he was so strong and kind and steady. Do you know that one day my car wouldn't start and people drove by for a long, long time, but it was Tanner who stopped to help? He's never treated me like a pariah. And there was this time at the diner when Rowan was fussing and he just stepped in and smoothed everything over. No one's ever done things like that for me, Maddy." She smiled, feeling a silly sentimentality. "He has this thing for doughnuts, did you know that? And he won't admit it, but I catch him looking at Rowan or holding her and he's not awkward or intimidated. I'd be crazy not to want a man like that in my life."

She was really laying it on thick, wasn't she? And yet every single word of it was true.

"You're sure you don't want to wait to get married?" Maddy asked. "I think it's the rush that is really throwing Ellen and John."

Laura shook her head. "I'm not popular here, and it's not like we'd have a big guest list. Something small and quiet is what we both want. We just want to get on with our lives, you know?"

"Still, it's a wedding. Surely, you want some romance to it. A month or two to plan things properly."

And give Tanner time to change his mind? Or for her to get cold feet? Or worst of all, for Spencer to get out of jail? "The wedding's set for just under three weeks," Laura replied, sitting a little straighter. "I've got lots of time to plan what I need. We already picked up the license and booked the JP."

"You need a dress. Rings. Flowers."

At this point, Laura's heart hurt. She didn't want this to be real. She felt guilty enough as it was, without the trappings of a real wedding, no matter how simple. "Really, Maddy. I'm just going to wear something in my closet. Or something I can wear again."

Maddy sat down and considered Laura for a long time. Rowan was playing happily, thanks to a full belly, dry diaper, and another hour before nap time. Maddy's face softened as she looked at the little girl, then back to Laura again.

"She's beautiful. She's got your nose and eyes. Even if the color isn't the same, the shape of them is."

"Thank you."

Maddy sighed. "Laura, you shouldn't feel like you have to sneak away like you've done something wrong. Why not have a new dress? A pretty bouquet?"

It's an extravagance for a farce, she wanted to reply, but held her tongue.

"Surely your parents, your grandparents…"

"My parents are in California now, and won't be coming up. Gram and Gramps, though…"

"Will expect you to look like a bride. Where are you having the ceremony?"

Once again Laura shrugged. "We haven't decided yet."

"Maybe you can have it at the ranch."

Laura was stricken by the suggestion. A guilty conscience was a terrible thing.

"Or below the library, at the gazebo, you know the place?" Maddy's smile widened. "Think about it. If there are only a few people, everyone can be beneath the roof if the weather isn't ideal. And if it's sunny, you've got a beautiful setting for pictures at no charge. You just have to reserve it with the town office."

Laura's throat tightened, touched by Maddy's acceptance and enthusiasm. "Why are you doing this? Everyone in Gibson thinks you have a big reason to hate me. And we've never been friends. Even without the affair, I was Gavin's high school girlfriend. It should still be awkward as hell."

"I'm doing it because you've had a rough time and you told me the truth when you didn't have to. And because we're probably going to be sisters-in-law and I'd like it to be so that family gatherings are fun."

Laura shook her head. "You have a very forgiving nature."

"I have a wonderful man who loves me and makes me see the world a little bit brighter than I did a few months ago. Please, Laura. If you love Tanner, give him a real wedding day to remember. His last one was such a farce and hurt him so badly."

Her words had the opposite effect than she'd intended. For the second time, Tanner's wedding was going to be a farce. He'd given up, hadn't he? He didn't believe in happy ever after and all that stuff. When he'd said he wasn't giving up anything to marry her, he'd meant it.

The thought made her sad, because deep down, she still believed in love. She still had a flicker of hope despite all that had happened. Tanner didn't. He was prepared to be completely pragmatic about the whole thing.

Briefly, she considered a wedding with a few more frills, but then what would be the point? It wouldn't change anything.

"I'll talk to Tanner," she promised. "It's his wedding, too, and he should have a say."

"Just consider it," Maddy said, folding her hands in her lap. "You can still have something quiet and small with very little fuss. It's just a few little touches. I think it would reassure John and Ellen, too."

"I'll think about it." She already was. The suggestion of the gazebo was a good one. They had to have it somewhere, after all. It wasn't as if they would get married here in her living room.

There was a long pause where the atmosphere became slightly uncomfortable again. Maddy looked as though she wanted to say something, and her hands fidgeted in her lap, but she was holding her tongue. Laura knew she should probably let it go, or change the subject, but curiosity got the best of her. "Maddy, if you've got something more to say, please say it."

Rowan spun in her saucer, the whirring sound of it occupying the silence for a few seconds.

"You had Rowan less than six months ago. It's not a long time from courtship to wedding. And no one knew you were seeing each other. It's so rushed. Are you absolutely sure this is what you want, Laura? That it's what's best for you and Rowan and for Tanner? Marriage is for a lifetime."

Except when it's not, Laura thought. She was tempted to explain, but held back. Maddy wouldn't be the last to question their motives. And it wasn't as if Laura had ever done anything to really earn their trust. She'd let everyone believe she'd had an extramarital affair for months. Even the reason for the secret was enough to wreck her credibility. What kind of person got pregnant with a drug pusher's baby?

And that line of thinking did absolutely nothing to prop up her already fragile confidence.

Except Tanner knew. And he was still beside her. Maybe not at this exact minute, but he was willing to help her when she needed it most. Despite her mistakes.

"I'm sure," she whispered. And with those words she silently promised herself that she'd never give Tanner a reason to regret his decision.

TANNER SIGHED HEAVILY as he climbed the front steps. He hadn't had time to change and there was blood on his uniform shirt. He was dog-tired and couldn't get the image of Carson Baxter out of his head.

What he really wanted right now was some peace and quiet, a hot shower, and a stiff drink. The last few days had been an adjustment, living at Laura's place, but they were managing all right. She was quieter than he expected, and he caught her looking at him sometimes with a strange expression on her face, but then she'd smile and go on doing something else.

If the worst thing about the move was missing his mom's cooking, he figured they were doing okay.

He wrinkled his nose. The windows were open and a strange, acrid smell wafted outside. It wasn't a scent he could place, but it sure didn't smell good. His already sensitive stomach turned over as he opened the door and the aroma grew stronger.

The kitchen was definitely not peaceful or orderly. A rolling pin and dirty mixing bowls sat on the table, some sort of strange batter stuck to the sides. Flour was everywhere, and on the stove was a still-smoking

roaster. He did a quick check to make sure it wasn't
still on the burner. It wasn't.

Beside the stove, he spotted the cause of the smell.
It was a pile of what he thought must be doughnuts,
but they were unlike any that he'd ever seen in his
life. Dark brown, lumpy bits of dough that…well. His
stomach turned again.

And where were Laura and the baby? The car was
out front so they had to be here somewhere. A horrible thought popped into his head. Had something
happened to Rowan that had caused Laura to forget
the hot fat in the roaster? He hurried from the kitchen,
calling out for her.

"Laura? Laura, are you okay?"

He rushed right past the living room to the bedrooms, but her soft voice came from behind him. "In
here."

She was in the rocker next to the TV, tucked away
in a corner of the living room. Rowan wasn't in her
lap. It was just her, sitting there with tears streaking
down her face.

"What is it? What's happened? Is Rowan okay?" He
rushed to her and knelt before the chair. "Is it Spence?
Laura honey, what's going on?"

Her lower lip wobbled. "She's napping. I—I tried
t-t-to make you doughnuts b-because I know they're
your favorites." She took a breath. "Nothing went right.
The b-batter was weird and didn't hold together and
then I burned them, but when I took them out the i-in-
side was still ruuuunnny…" The last word was drawn
out with despair, but finally ended when she punctu-
ated the sentence with a sniff. "I—I'm so sorry, Tanner. I wanted to surprise you."

"So nothing's wrong? This is just about dough-nuts?" God, he was so relieved. With the mess in the kitchen, the silence and everything that had already happened today...not to mention the situation with Laura and how worried she was about her ex. He'd never experienced his heart freezing before, but that was what it had been like. As if it had stopped and everything had turned cold.

Another sniff. "I wanted to do something nice for you."

He dropped his head, unsure how much more of a roller coaster he could take today. "Goddammit, don't scare me like that again, okay?"

She flinched. "I didn't mean to scare you. I—I was just in here feeling sorry for myself. I'll go clean up the mess. I didn't mean to upset you. I'm really sorry."

It occurred to him how much she was apologizing and it made him feel like a heel. He softened his voice. "Stop saying you're sorry. It's fine, really. I've just had a hell of a day, that's all. I'm all wound up and nowhere to put it."

She placed her hand on the side of his face, and he looked up abruptly. Her face was still streaked and her eyes red, but there was concern in them, too.

"What is it?" She looked at his shirt, and the color drained from her face. "You've got blood on your shirt."

"We got a call midmorning." He closed his eyes, wishing he could unsee the scene. "It was a bad one."

"Do you want to talk about it?"

He shook his head quickly. "No."

Her thumb rubbed against his cheek. "Okay. Then

let's get you out of your uniform. Unless you're still on call."

"No." His throat felt raw. "Not… I mean, someone else is covering for us." It had been Sean McEachern on call with him today. They'd been debriefed and then relieved.

"Come on, then." The color had returned to Laura's face and erased the weakness he'd seen only moments before. She grasped his hands and stood, urging him to his feet. *Damn, he was wobbly.*

Laura got up from the rocker and held his hand as she led him down the hall. Tanner felt an unfamiliar tightening in his chest, which was at odds with the numb sensation in his legs and arms. It was like an out-of-body experience, following her, and that was when he realized why he'd been sent home for the rest of the day. He'd functioned through it all. The call, the debriefing at the hospital, everything…but now it was setting in and his body started to shake.

"Sit down, Tanner."

Her soft voice commanded him and he obeyed, not knowing what else to do. He sat at the foot of the bed, staring at her as she went to a couple of drawers, looking for a T-shirt. She took one out and then stood before him, reached for the buttons on his shirt and began undoing them, one by one.

"Let's get your shirt changed first. I'll call my grandma and see what she suggests for getting the stains out."

Blood. It was blood. And that was only a small part of it.

Her soft, cool fingers pushed the shirt off his shoulders and she tossed it onto the bed behind her. As gently as if she were dressing Rowan, she helped him put on the soft cotton T-shirt.

"Can you stand up, Tanner?"

"Huh? Oh. Yes."

"Do you have a pair of sweats anywhere?"

He nodded numbly. "Shelf in the closet."

It was the oddest sensation, having a woman un-buckle his pants without there being any sexual over-tones. She was simply gentle and efficient, helping him take them off, putting his feet through the legs of the sweats and pulling them up to rest on his hips.

"Better?"

He nodded, though he knew it wasn't. He was try-ing so hard not to shake right now. He didn't want to be that weak in front of her. This was all so stupid. He'd been working as an EMT for some time. He'd been on calls for vehicle accidents, heart attacks, strokes and yes, even Laura's baby. But today…

He shivered all over.

She urged him back on the bed, and he let her, which surprised him. "I'm fine," he protested. "I'm just coming down from the adrenaline. Give me a minute."

"Okay," she agreed. "And I think you should come down from the adrenaline by being horizontal. You're a lot bigger than me, Tanner." She smiled at him. "If you tip over on me I'll be squashed."

"Just for a minute, though."

"Fair enough. Would you like some water or some-thing? I can't burn that."

He tried to smile. "Water's great. Thanks."

She disappeared for a moment and he forced him-self to take deep breaths. He'd been running on au-topilot for the last few hours, and then his adrenaline had spiked again when he thought something might be wrong with Laura and Rowan. Truth was, he was all over the map and he was smart enough to know his body—and his fiancée—was telling him to hold up for a bit and find his feet again.

Finding his feet was something that Carson Baxter would never do again.

Tanner closed his eyes, but nothing erased the image of that kid.

Laura came back and sat on the edge of the bed, holding the glass of water. "Here," she said quietly. "Drink slowly."

He took a sip, but then put the glass on the table beside the bed. "I'm okay."

"It must have been really horrible, huh?"

He nodded. "Yuh. Worst I've been on. It's just catching up with me, is all."

She waited a few seconds and then asked hesitantly, "Was anyone killed, Tanner?"

This time he couldn't get his voice to work. He nodded.

"Oh," she said, a quiet lament. "I'm sorry."

He might have been able to reply. Might have found his voice and said something strong and restorative, except Laura leaned forward and slid her arms around his middle and put her head against his chest. He was leaning against the headboard, and the scroll of the wood dug into the back of his head. He welcomed the sensation, let it anchor him, let the feel of her embrace anchor him, too. He put his hand along her back and felt the warmth of her skin through her thin top. And then the next thing he knew, he'd reached out and gathered her close and pulled her on to his lap, holding her tight.

She didn't fight. She simply let him hold her as if she knew that was exactly what he needed. And he absorbed her warmth and strength until he began to feel whole again.

"Do you want to talk about it now?" she finally asked.

He sighed. "No. But it'll be on the news, in the paper. You'll hear about it anyway."

"It was an accident?" she prodded gently, her hand still rubbing reassuringly on his back.

"Yeah. Out at Baxter's place. Do you know where that is?"

He couldn't tell for sure, since she was still snuggled up against him, but he thought her head movement indicated no.

"It's a ranch south of town. The call came in just after ten." He took a deep breath and just said it. "A tractor rolled over and killed the driver."

"Oh God," she said, squeezing him tight.

"He was fifteen."

Those three words settled in the room, heavy with sorrow and the loss of all the possibilities that would have been ahead for that young life. "Oh, Tanner," she said, and for a moment or two he just held on.

"Sean and I...we worked on him for a long time. He wasn't dead when we got there, but he was..." Tanner halted when his voice broke a bit. He cleared his throat. "He was hurt real bad. And his dad and a couple of the hands were standing there crying and we had to just focus and not see the kid, just the job."

"Which is impossible, of course."

He nodded. "We were almost to the hospital when we lost him. They worked on him awhile there, but the internal bleeding was too much. And now I can't get that kid's face out of my head."

She pulled back out of his arms a bit, and he drank in the sight of her face, so beautiful and alive. He'd needed her today, he realized. He'd thought about going home to the place he'd lived all his life, but instead he'd come here. To her. He wasn't sure he was comfortable with that, but he'd think about it later. Right now he was just grateful he was where he needed to be.

"I shouldn't be dumping all this on you," he said.

"We're friends, and I'm glad you did." She slid her fingers down to his hands and squeezed. "I've been feeling like this arrangement is so one-sided. You being there to help me out of trouble, but me offering little in return. If I can help you with this, it makes me feel useful. Like... I'm giving you something back." She sighed. "Like I actually have something to offer."

"You have more than you realize," he murmured, tightening his hands on hers. "Talking has helped, actually." He paused. "And letting me hold you. I think I needed a nice, warm human being this afternoon."

When her lips turned up in a sweet smile, the ugliness of the day seemed to melt away. "Maybe we should get you a dog," she joked.

"I said human being," he replied, but he smiled in return, feeling some of his muscles relax.

He hadn't realized how tightly he'd been holding himself until he started to let go.

Chapter Eleven

As Tanner relaxed, he started to notice other things, too. Like how her coppery hair set off her creamy skin; her eyes were a deep shade of blue that seemed bottomless, her bottom lip was fuller than the top and she had a habit of nibbling on it when she was nervous.

It would be the easiest thing in the world to reach for her right now. To sink his hands into that gorgeous waterfall of hair, to kiss her soft lips and pull her body close against his. Her thumb rubbed against the top of his hand, and his body responded to the simple touch, fueling a desire so profound it shocked him. He didn't just want to have sex. He thought of how guileless she was, how unaware of her own attractiveness, and wanted to show her the way he saw her.

Tanner wanted to make love to her. It was very different from scratching an itch or fulfilling a fantasy. He wanted to worship her body with his.

But he wouldn't. The unexpected emotions that prompted these thoughts were the same ones that reminded him of the fragility of their situation, of the need for care and caution. After their last kiss, he'd agreed they wouldn't complicate things by becoming physically involved.

She needed to be able to trust him to keep his word.

So he pushed his libido aside—with difficulty—and focused instead on the unique practicality of the situation.

"Let's change the subject to something happier," he suggested, sliding back a little and stretching out his legs so their pose wasn't so intimate. "Anything new with plans?"

She took his cue, thankfully, and slid her fingers away from his. "Actually, yes. I looked into a site for the ceremony. We can have it at the gazebo on the riverbank, you know the one? Just beyond the library. I checked with the town hall and apparently we can book it for an hour that Sunday afternoon."

He nodded. "That sounds nice."

"Maddy made a point that we shouldn't just have it in the living room. That we should do something at least modestly matrimonial."

His eyebrows shot up. "Maddy?"

"She stopped by a few days ago. After you'd talked to her and Cole."

Ah yes. The conversation that had been strained at best, though they'd put on a good face the moment he'd brought up that he knew they knew the truth. Their concerns had been the same as his parents', and he had been on the brink of telling them the truth. It bothered him to lie to his brother, in particular.

While it had been difficult to keep up the pretense of a real marriage, it hadn't been hard at all to stand up for Laura. His defense of her probably went a long way to his family reconciling themselves to the wedding.

Maybe they weren't in love. But neither was Laura opportunistic or callous. He was unexpectedly touched by her words today about feeling helpful and needed. She'd made room for him in her house. In her life. That was far bigger than a piece of paper.

"I suppose people are going to expect a certain, I don't know, sense of occasion." He floundered over the words. He wasn't good at this sort of thing. "The park sounds really nice. You should have a new dress, and one for Rowan, too. Order a few flowers. Get your hair done. When was the last time you pampered yourself a little?"

She wasn't looking at him now and he got the sense he'd said something wrong. "Laura? What is it? Did I say something wrong? You don't have to do those things if you don't want to. I just thought… Never mind. I'm probably an idiot."

When she looked at him, he swore her eyes were damp, though no tears glistened on her lashes or touched her cheeks. "It's not that. It's a lovely idea. Except, well, we're at the point where we're honest with each other, right?"

"You did my laundry yesterday." He smiled at her. "You've officially folded my underwear. We're living together. I think honesty might be a good idea."

He was gratified to see her smile a bit.

"It's two things, really," she admitted, and he noticed she picked at a cuticle with her fingernail. "I don't really have the money to go do all those things. And even if I did…" She swallowed. "A bride should have a sister or girlfriends or someone to go on a shopping trip like that. The thought of going alone is gross."

A reminder of her outcast status in the community. He got it. It was that way because of the sacrifice she'd made thinking it would be best for her daugh-

ter. "None of your old school friends have stayed in
touch?" After all, Laura had grown up here. Surely
she'd stayed friends with someone.

"A few did at first, until it was obvious I was pregnant. When everyone thought it was Gavin's, they
stopped calling."

"I'm sorry."

She made a "what can you do?" face. "Even if I'd
said Rowan wasn't his, I doubt anyone would have
believed me. So I kept my head down and my mouth
shut."

The thought of dress-shopping was not a happy
one, but neither was the idea of her feeling so incredibly lonely. The people in this town needed a kick in
the rear.

"I'll go with you. And I'll pick up the tab. I'm pretty
sure I can afford a dress and a few flowers or something."

"Tanner, that's generous of you, but I can't let you
do that."

Pride. He was starting to understand that she
seemed to be keeping a running tab in her head. "Listen, keep the receipts if you like. When your business
is up and going, you can pay me back, if you feel that
strongly about it."

He didn't have any intention of taking her money,
but she didn't need to know that.

"You really want to go shopping?" She raised an
eyebrow at him.

"Why not?" He had a suit, so he shrugged. "Maybe
I'll get a new tie."

Her face lit up. Just a bit, but he knew he'd done the
right thing by suggesting it.

"Let me know what day is good for you. I'll work around your schedule."

"If I tell Cole I'm taking a day for wedding plans, he won't think anything of it. We'll go into the city. Have lunch. Make a day of it. Maybe Monday? I'm on call again this weekend." And he'd deal with that when the time came. He loved his EMT work. He wasn't about to abandon it because of one horrible call.

"Okay," she said, nodding. "But nothing fancy. I'd like something nice that I can wear again."

He wasn't sure if that was a practical streak or if she really thought she didn't deserve any better. He hoped it was the first.

She touched his knee. "Thank you, Tanner. Are you feeling any better now?"

He was. There was a lingering heaviness when he thought about the day's events, but the shock and shakes had worn off from the distraction she'd provided. He suspected she'd done it deliberately, clever woman.

"I am. Now that the adrenaline's worn off, I'm kind of crashing, though. Man, I'm so tired."

"Have a sleep, then. Rowan will be up soon and I should go clean up the disaster that was the doughnuts." She crawled off the bed and stretched.

"Laura?" He looked up at her, felt helplessly as though he was starting to care far too much. "About the doughnuts. Really, you don't have to try so hard. I appreciate the effort." He sent her a crooked smile, because they both knew what a mess it had turned out to be. "But seriously, you don't have to be anything other than who you are. That's enough. I want you to remember that, okay?"

Her gaze touched his, and he felt the strange thump in his chest that seemed to happen whenever she looked at him with her eyes all soft and her lips slightly parted.

"You're a good man," she murmured. "Thank you for saying that, Tanner."

She slipped out of the room before he could say anything more, and he closed his eyes and sank back against the pillows. She'd thanked him for saying it, but he got the impression she didn't believe it.

Dammit. He was only supposed to like her. What the hell was he doing falling for her anyway?

LAURA KNEW SHE had no right to be so excited.

It wasn't a real wedding. She wasn't shopping for a real wedding dress. And yet the idea of going shopping, of buying something new and pretty was so exhilarating. And something for Rowan, too, she determined. She could afford to buy her daughter a little frilly dress for the ceremony.

By nine o'clock Monday morning, they were ready to go. Tanner had gone to the ranch early to help with morning chores and catch up on some other odd jobs, but he'd promised to be back by nine-thirty.

Rowan was fed, bathed, and dressed in cute leggings and a ruffled top with a bonnet on her head that she kept picking at in boredom. Laura had dressed up, too, in the same dress she'd worn the night Tanner made his crazy proposal. On her feet were little sandals with kitten heels that she thought might work while trying on dresses. She had everything in the diaper bag, including a small dish containing some dry cereal that she'd recently started feeding to

Rowan. Now she was pacing, waiting for Tanner to come home, stopping in the hall mirror to check her lip gloss one more time.

It felt real. It had felt real ever since he came home last week, his shirt spattered with blood and heartbreak in his eyes. Something had changed that day, when he looked at her before going to sleep. He hadn't kissed her, hadn't done anything inappropriate. But there was a different closeness between them now. An awareness. Maybe it was wrong, maybe it was ill-advised, but it was there all the same. It would take a stronger woman than her to resist Tanner's gallantry.

He'd worked two more shifts on ambulance duty on the weekend, and she'd worried about him. He'd come home quiet and somewhat subdued, but on Saturday night, Rowan had been fussing a bit and he'd sat on the floor with her and played and seemed to come around. Lord help her, for a few minutes they'd actually felt like a little family.

Would it be so bad to pretend it was a tiny bit real?

A growl in the front yard announced the return of Tanner and his truck. They'd agreed to take her car today, since it was easier on gas and the car seat was already inside.

"You ready, darlin'?" she said to Rowan. "Gonna get you a new dress today. Mama, too."

Tanner bounded in, his face relaxed and smiling. "You're all ready to go. Excellent."

"Ro always has me up early. Plus, I think she's excited for shopping."

"Oh, she is, is she? I think her mama's the one who's excited."

"Maybe just a little."

"I thought we'd hit the mall in Great Falls, unless you want a specialty shop or something. I don't know much about dresses and stuff."

"The mall is fine. There's a JCPenney there." She was more than happy to go to the department store. Just having the day away from Gibson was enough.

"Let's go, then. I've got a hot chocolate for you in the car, and coffee for me. Thought we could use it for the drive."

Hot chocolate, and a shopping trip. Wasn't he full of surprises?

She smiled at him. He was all sexiness today, in dark jeans, boots and a clean shirt—had he changed at the ranch? And he was wearing a hat, his good one, clean and dust-free. The quintessential cowboy heading into the city to buy his girl a dress. If that wasn't swoon-worthy, what was?

It only took a minute to fasten Rowan in the back and head down the driveway. Laura waited to open her hot chocolate until they were on the highway, heading away from Gibson. To her amusement, Tanner took a sip of coffee and then reached down beside him for a paper sack.

She laughed. "Let me guess. Honey glazed?"

"You know me too well," he said, grinning and shoving half a doughnut into his mouth.

She was starting to, she realized.

When he'd swallowed the enormous bite, he glanced over at her. "Thanks for getting my uniform shirt clean, by the way. I don't think I thanked you before."

She smiled. "It wasn't me. I took it over to Gram's. She showed me how to get the stain out."

"Some home remedy or trick, I suppose," he commented, focusing on the road again.

She laughed lightly. "Actually, she had a stain stick. It worked great."

Tanner laughed.

It seemed like no time at all before they were at the mall. She removed Rowan from her seat and put her in a little stroller, small enough to be convenient for the aisles of the department store. They headed straight for the women's clothing, and Laura noticed some of the sidelong looks that followed them. It was so different from Gibson. The looks were warm and approving, rather than judgmental. As though they were looking at the three of them as a family. It was nice, and she wondered again at the wisdom of staying in Gibson. Maybe in another few years, she'd be able to afford to move outside the town.

This marriage would give her freedom she couldn't otherwise afford. Not just from the name change, but the sharing of expenses.

It was a sobering thought.

They made their way through women's wear to the fancy dresses. Laura stared at the clothing on the hangers and her heart sank. There were actual wedding dresses here. Oh, nothing over the top, but long white dresses appropriate for weddings. Once upon a time she'd dreamt of such things.

"Do you see anything you like?"

She swallowed, her throat working against the emotion lodged there. "Tanner, I don't think I can wear a long white dress."

"It's up to you, but I got the impression that the

whole 'white' thing doesn't really matter much any-more." He smiled at her. "Get something you like."

The gowns were beautiful, but not right. "Maybe there's something over here, in the cocktail dress section," she said, leading him away. Rowan peered around curiously, intrigued by the lights and colors.

It wasn't long before she saw a few dresses that she considered appropriate. There was a white one, short and strapless yet modest. She let go of her "no white" idea because the dress was so cute. Then she found a periwinkle satin-y number and a blush-pink lace dress with a ribbon sash, which she adored but wondered how it would look with her red hair.

"Will you watch Ro while I try these on?" she asked, her stomach curling with excited nerves. The dresses were all so pretty. Not cheap, but not overly expensive, either. Maybe she'd even have occasion to wear it again, though she didn't know where. Maybe if Cole and Maddy got married...

She slipped into the dressing room.

First up was the white dress. She liked it a lot, but the bust was a bit tight, and with it being strapless, she wasn't sure what would happen with her breasts, since she was still nursing.

The periwinkle one had a nice style, but the col-oring was all wrong with her hair and complexion. She looked completely washed out. She took it off as quickly as she'd put it on.

"Everything okay in there?" came Tanner's voice.

"Just a little longer. Is that okay?"

He chuckled warmly. "Take your time. Ro's chew-ing on her giraffe."

She slipped into the pink dress and zipped it up. The

moment she turned to the mirror she knew. The pale pink was subtle enough that it didn't clash with her hair, and the lace overskirt was incredibly feminine. Plus, she didn't feel as if her bust was on display. The satin ribbon at the waist added a touch of class and formality that would suit a wedding just fine.

She wouldn't feel as guilty wearing pink.

"I think I've found it," she called out.

"Let's see," Tanner suggested.

"No." She clung to at least a little bit of wedding protocol. "It's bad luck."

His voice was close to the change room door. "Laura, we're not exactly conventional here."

She pressed her head against the door. "Tanner, please. I'd like to keep *something* a surprise. Okay?"

"Of course it's okay." His voice was soft. "You're sure you don't want to look at something else?"

She was sure. It fit perfectly and she felt pretty in it. "I'm sure. You'll learn me fairly quickly, Tanner. I'm kind of low maintenance."

He laughed. "Okay, then. We'll disappear for a minute while you come out."

She changed back into her regular clothes and reluctantly hung the dress on the hanger again. She took all three out, gave two to the saleslady to hang back up and then handed her the pink one to hold on to until they were ready to go. "I'm going to look for shoes and a dress for my daughter," she explained, looking longingly after the dress. She hadn't wanted to take it off.

She found Tanner and Rowan in the children's section. Tanner was staring at the ruffled items, and she hesitated for a moment, committing the image to memory. The lean, rugged cowboy surrounded by tiny lace and eyelet dresses and bloomers.

"Hi," she said, smiling and stepping forward. "Find anything you like?"

"I wouldn't know where to start." He had his hands on the handles of the stroller and Laura got all squishy inside.

"Well, babies are fun to buy for. Especially baby girls. Ruffles, cotton lace, frills and all that stuff." She ran her fingers over racks of adorable sets, but then found one rack with little pastel dresses. Her heart melted.

"Oh, look," she said. She picked up a white cotton lace dress with a pink sash. "Isn't this cute?"

"Look at this kid." He pointed at Rowan, who drooled over her plastic Sophie the Giraffe. "I challenge you to find anything that wouldn't be cute."

Laura browsed for longer than she'd taken with her own dress, but then she spotted a beautiful pink dress with a two-tiered pleated skirt and a little shrug that resembled rosebuds. It was perfect. With Rowan's dark hair and heavily lashed blue eyes, the pink would be amazing. And Laura already had the perfect pair of white soft shoes to put on her feet.

"This is the one," she said, holding it up.

Tanner looked down at her and her she went all mushy. "You went with the pink one for your dress, didn't you?"

She didn't want him to know for sure. "Well, it's not the periwinkle."

"You mean the purple-y one?"

She grinned. "Yeah. I did try on a white one, though."

He shook his head, his gaze steady on hers. "Nope. It's the pink one."

"What makes you say that?" she challenged, though she was loving every minute of the exchange.

"Because of the way your face looked when you took it off the rack. It got all... I don't know. Soft-looking. And now with the pink dress for Rowan..."

She couldn't remember the last time she'd been this happy.

"Do you think I could look at shoes?"

"A new dress needs new shoes. Or so Maddy told me."

Maddy. An unexpected ally.

The day was like a fairy tale. They went to the shoe department and she found a pair of simple blush-colored pumps. When they were done, they headed back to the first saleslady and Tanner pulled out his bank card and paid for the three items.

"Tanner, thank you. I promise I'll pay you back."

"It's my pleasure," he assured her.

She had a sudden idea. "Hey, you know how you said you might get a new tie?"

He nodded.

"Will you let me get that for you? As a wedding present? I know it's not exactly equal—"

"But it would make you feel better," he finished for her.

"Well, yeah."

"I'd be honored, Laura." He let go of the stroller for a moment and reached for her hand. "I don't want us to have to keep track of every penny, you know. We're both getting something out of this arrangement. For what it's worth, I'm happy being out of the house. It was past time for me to do it."

"So, a tie. What color is your suit?"

He shrugged. "Black."

She laughed. "Of course it is. Black suit, white shirt, right? Okay."

They detoured over to men's wear and stopped at a table with an assortment of silk ties. Laura considered dove gray, black, white, but in the end she chose the light pink one. She picked it up and held it to his shirt front. "What do you say? Are you man enough to wear pink?"

He laughed. "It's a tie. It's not like you're going to dress me in a tutu. I think I can handle it."

He was so easygoing. Did he realize how amazing that made him? Tanner worried about the big stuff and didn't sweat the small stuff. Laura admired him for that. More than he knew. "Then I will buy it for you. A proper wedding tie."

It was a little thing, but she took pride in taking it to the sales counter and paying for it herself. She tucked the little bag into the larger one containing their dresses and her shoes. "Well," she said, "it's hardly noon, and we're done already. What's next?"

He patted his belly. "I'm out of doughnuts. I was thinking we could grab some lunch somewhere before heading back." He chuckled. "You're an efficient shopper, Laura. I was prepared to spend the day in lots of stores and a lot of time outside change rooms."

"You learn to be economical with your time when you have a baby," she replied, gazing at Rowan in the stroller.

"She's been so good today."

"Sleeping better lately, too. It might be because I've started her on some solids." Thank God for rice cereal.

"So, what do you feel like? Mexican? Asian? Sandwiches? Greek?"

It was all fast food choices yet it felt extravagant just the same. "Asian? Is that okay with you?"

He laughed. "I'll eat anything."

"Even my cooking?" she teased.

He grinned. "Well, maybe not your doughnuts, but you haven't poisoned me yet."

At the small restaurant, Laura scanned the menu. When was the last time she'd had takeout like this? She decided on a small order of chicken lo mein and a bottle of water; Tanner ordered a bigger combination meal. Seating was limited, but he snagged them a spot in the corner, and while Tanner waited for their order, Laura put Rowan on her lap and opened a jar of pureed bananas. She'd expressed enough milk for a bottle as well, so she'd be spared any awkward moments during their shopping trip. By the time Tanner returned to the table with the tray, Rowan had gobbled up almost a third of the jar of bananas and was settled happily with the bottle.

"Wow, you didn't waste any time." Tanner divvied up napkins and forks, and then considerately opened her water, since her hands were fairly occupied.

"I figured I'd feed her before she started screaming about it," Laura said. "I guess I should have started her on some solids earlier. She loves her cereal, and bananas and applesauce."

"It's not like you've ever done this before," he noted, digging his fork into a mound of fried rice. "She looks pretty happy to me."

Indeed, Rowan was drinking away happily, and Laura was having a great time. No one knew them here. They were simply a couple out shopping, enjoying lunch and relaxing. There was nothing to worry about in this moment, and it was a glorious feeling. "You look happy, too," Tanner said. He speared a piece of saucy chicken and popped it into his mouth.

"I am. It's been a lovely morning."

"It's just shopping." He chuckled a little, but she shook her head. How could she possibly explain that it was far more than a little shopping? What it meant that he'd taken his time and hard-earned money to make this possible? She felt as though she didn't deserve any of it.

And she was starting to wish that it were real, that Tanner did care for her and her for him. The last part wasn't much of a stretch; any woman would be lucky to have such a man on her side.

"Here," Tanner said, putting down his fork. "Let me take her for a few minutes. You've hardly managed to eat anything."

"Are you sure?"

He nodded. "I've held her a few times now and we're getting used to each other." He held out his arms and she shifted, taking the empty bottle from Rowan's lips and wiping a dribble of milk from her chin.

Laura put Rowan in his arms and watched as he cradled her daughter close, as gently as if she were spun glass. Her pulse thumped as she handed him the flannel blanket. "She might have some gas," she said.

"We got it covered, don't we, short stuff?" he asked the baby. Rowan stared up at him with wide and trusting eyes. Then she burped, dribbling some milk over her chin, which Tanner deftly wiped up with the flannel.

Laura took the precious opportunity to have two free hands. She forked up some lo mein and the flavors exploded in her mouth. "Mmm, this is so good," she mumbled, swallowing.

"Really? It's not gourmet, you know." Tanner's eyebrow was raised in amusement.

"Doesn't matter. One, I didn't cook it." She scooped more on her fork and met his gaze. "Two, it's been so long since I had Chinese food. This is a real treat, Tanner. Thanks."

She shoveled more into her mouth, chewing happily.

"I'm glad." Tanner bounced his knee a bit, keeping Rowan happy. "You deserve to get out now and again."

"And the dresses and stuff, too. I promise I'll pay you back. Do you know I have my website nearly ready to go? I'm putting the finishing touches on my submit-for-quote forms to make them as straightforward as possible. Once I do that, I can start doing up proposal packages and really going after some business."

"That's great." He was smiling and it was so nice to feel someone's approval. She hadn't realized how terribly she'd missed such a simple thing, but clearly she had. Her work at her last job had been satisfactory and her boss had always been pleased, but it wasn't that this time. She respected Tanner's opinion, and having him support her choices meant more than he knew.

She scraped the bottom of the carton and sat back in her chair. "I'm stuffed. What should we do now?"

"I took the whole day off. Is there anything else you need to do for the wedding?

There was one thing in particular, but as much as

they'd shopped together today and were treating the wedding as a simple event, she found she couldn't bring it up. It was a sensitive topic and she wasn't sure how to broach without feeling terrible about disregarding the sanctity of marriage or having it seem that she was making more of it than there was.

But someday soon, they would need to talk about what they were going to do for wedding rings.

Chapter Twelve

In the end, Laura lost the nerve to bring up the subject of rings. Instead, she took a day and went to the city herself, and picked out what she hoped would be the right size for Tanner in a plain gold band. There was no way she was going to ask him to buy his own wedding ring.

The weather was nearly summer-like, and when she got returned from town she found him on the front step in a T-shirt and jeans, a tool belt slung low over his hips. "You're home early," she called out, realizing how very domestic it sounded.

"I wanted to fix the front step, and in another few days we'll be ready for our first cut of hay. I'll be working longer days at the ranch and probably won't have time."

"Oh." She'd miss him being home in the evenings, but she was guessing it would be close to dark when he got home. Maybe he was regretting leaving the ranch. If he lived there, he wouldn't have any travel time.

But she didn't say that because she didn't want it to sound as if she didn't want him at her house when she did—so very much.

He stood and she saw the way his muscles filled out

the light cotton of his T-shirt, how his jeans sat on his hips, the waistband just above the leather of the tool belt. The wedding ring she'd bought was cushioned in a little ring box in her purse, and Rowan sat on her arm, her small bonneted head looking all around. Laura noticed Rowan following the progress of a butterfly and she smiled. Lord, she was precious. For all of life's troubles, she wouldn't trade her little one for anything in the world.

"She's looking cute today." Laura hadn't realized that Tanner had come down the few steps to meet her, and she started when she realized how close he was.

"I have to say, I love shopping for the cute little clothes. Sometimes we just go to the secondhand store in town. Babies outgrow things so quickly that they're hardly ever worn out. Stained a little sometimes, but still in good shape."

"My mom always said the best bleach in the world was sunlight."

Laura nodded. "Gram said that, too, the day I took your shirt over to wash. We hung it on her line."

"Let me help you up the steps. I still have a tread to replace. But it should be much sturdier for you."

The third step, the one just before the small landing, was missing, but Laura could see the fresh yellow-y brown boards on the other steps and noted how solid they were beneath her feet, with no creaks or tilts. When she got to the second to-the-top step, Tanner put his hands on her waist and simply lifted her—and Rowan—the eighteen inches to the top.

"Oh!" She couldn't stop the light exclamation. Goodness, he'd done that as if she weighed nothing at all, when she knew very well she was still carrying a good portion of her baby weight, as well as her baby.

"There you go. I shouldn't be long here. What's for supper?" He winked. He asked that almost every night, always teasing. Her lack of cooking skills had become a bit of a running joke.

"Spaghetti," she replied. This was something she could manage halfway decently by using canned goods for the sauce. There was a salad kit in the fridge, which only required her to dump everything into a bowl. She'd picked up sugar cookies as a treat for him to have for dessert.

She put Rowan to play in a playpen she'd found at a garage sale the past weekend. Her daughter was now starting to scooch herself along in a prequel to proper crawling. Humming softly to herself, Laura browned a little hamburger in a pan and then added a couple of jars of sauce. A quick taste proved the sauce to be somewhat bland, so she added seasonings to spice it up a bit. Then she put water on to boil for the pasta, dug out a salad bowl and listened to Tanner's random sounds of sawing and hammering.

When the pasta was cooked, she drained it and poured it into a big bowl, poured the sauce over top and put it on the table along with the salad. She went to the door and stuck her head outside. "Tanner? Dinner's ready."

"Great. I got the last step fixed and I'm starving."

He unbuckled the tool belt and Laura tried not to follow the movement of his hands with her eyes. She failed. When she glanced up, he was watching her with an amused expression.

Her cheeks flared. "It's getting cold."

"Certainly. Just let me wash up."

When he'd come back from the bathroom, she was seated at the table, scooping a big helping of pasta onto his plate. "So," she said, determined to start a normal conversation. "You're starting haying. Does that mean the wedding is bad timing?"

"Not really." He picked up his fork, took his plate from her fingers. "Thanks. Anyway, my mom and dad never work on Sunday. Well, I shouldn't say never. If the weather forecast is bad, we might work right through. But other than daily chores? Mom and Dad always believed in a day of rest. During our busiest times, that was always our day for family."

"That sounds nice," Laura said, loving the way his family sounded more and more.

"When I was younger, it was a pain in the ass. Now I appreciate it, though. Everyone needs some down-time."

"I officially invited my grandparents," she said, taking the salad utensils and putting some lettuce on her plate. "With your folks and Cole and Maddy, that makes six. Is there anyone else you want to tell?"

He shrugged. "I've got friends, but we're keeping this small, right? Cole will be our witness. How about you?"

She thought of a few friends she'd reconnected with when she came back to town, and who'd then awk-wardly found excuses to back out of plans when the rumors about Gavin started spreading. "No," she said, quite definite. "Let's just have the eight of us. Nine, including Ro." She smiled. "Perfect number for in-side the gazebo."

"Hey," he said, "this spaghetti isn't half-bad."

"A rousing endorsement."

He laughed. "I mean it. You're getting better."

From anyone else it would sound patronizing. From Tanner, though—she knew it was a genuine compliment, and she took it as such.

After dinner, she offered him a couple of cookies and a fresh cup of coffee. While she cleaned up the mess, Tanner headed back outside, and to her surprise, she saw him wielding a paintbrush. He was painting the railings a lovely, brilliant white. It was going to look amazing. It warmed her heart in ways she couldn't explain. While Tanner hadn't given her actual rent for this month, he'd taken her shopping for wedding stuff and picked up the tab. He'd bought groceries, changed the oil in her car and filled it up and now fixed the steps. That was worth far more than rent.

He kept up his work and she finished the dishes, fed Rowan pureed sweet potato and peas, then gave her a bath and dressed her in clean, fuzzy pajamas. The evening was turning soft, the light muted through the windows, when she finally sat in the rocker in the living room to nurse Rowan before bed.

Tanner came in and called out, "Laura, I'm going to clean the paintbrush and stuff down in the basement, okay?"

"Sure."

She'd started to fall asleep in the chair, and only roused when she heard Tanner's steps coming up from the basement. Rowan was sound asleep in her arms; Laura awkwardly set her clothing straight as best she could before he came into the room.

He stopped in the doorway and rested his shoulder on the frame. "Out like a light."

Laura nodded.

"Looks like her mama's about ready, as well. Did you fall asleep again?"

It was the *again* that got her. It spoke of habit, of intimacy. She already knew she would miss him when they went their separate ways. How hard would it be months from now when they lived together for so long?

"I might have dozed off for a few minutes," she confessed. "You painted the railings."

"A first coat. It needs a second because the wood soaks up the paint so much. But it's a start."

"Thank you so much."

He pushed away from the frame, pulled up a foot stool and sat in front of her. He touched a single, rough finger to the soft hair above Rowan's ear, the ghost of a smile flickering over his face. "Laura, I wasn't sure what to expect when I moved in. I know we said it would be like a trial period. The wedding's a little over a week away now. I know we've made the plans and everything, but I wanted to make sure this is still what you want."

"Is it what you want?"

His gaze held hers. "Yes. Very much. I like coming home to you. To you both."

Her heart leaped. "I like having you here, too. It feels... I don't know. More like a home somehow."

"I'm glad."

"I know you're busy, and I want to thank you again for everything you've been doing around here."

He put his hand on hers. "It's something I can contribute, and I like doing it. Otherwise I might feel like I was merely a boarder. Know what I mean?"

She nodded, understanding completely.

"Besides, you make a man want to do things for you. When you smile at me and say thanks, it's good for my ego." His grin widened, and his fingers tightened on hers. Before she knew what was happening, they'd twined with hers so they weren't just touching, but holding hands. Really holding hands.

She was no innocent girl. And he certainly wasn't an innocent man. He'd been married and she'd borne another man's child. But in that moment, when their fingers meshed and their eyes met, something changed. Something pure, and yes, even innocent. Something big and important. For the first time, she let her feelings flood her heart. She didn't just like Tanner. She loved him.

It was so not part of the plan. She wasn't supposed to fall in love with him. And if she told him? Everything would be ruined. They couldn't get married if he knew the truth, so she determined to keep it buried deep inside. For as long as it took.

He leaned forward and kissed her, lightly, a whisper of a kiss that was far more devastating in its tenderness than the most passionate of embraces. She was in real danger here, torn between wanting to follow her heart and doing what she knew she must.

When the kiss ended, she sat back and smiled. "Well, we should be fine on the day. No awkwardness."

His gaze cooled a little, and understanding flickered in his eyes. But she saw something else, too. She saw that she wasn't fooling anyone.

Rowan shifted in her arms, perhaps uncomfortable from the slight squeeze of moments before.

"You're tired. You should put Rowan to bed and head there yourself."

And away from him. It wasn't a bad idea. She'd read. Or stare at the ceiling and marvel at how she was incredibly talented at getting herself into impossible situations.

He was far enough away that she could get up, holding Rowan close in her arms. But she needed to slide past him to go toward the hall and the bedrooms, and he didn't stand or move aside, either.

She brushed by him and ducked into the bedroom, exhaling a breath. She then turned back and leaned out a little. "Good night, Tanner."

"Good night, Laura."

Maybe one of these days she'd get up the courage to bring up what was happening between them. Today definitely wasn't that day, she thought with a rueful laugh as she lay down on top of her bed.

She hadn't brushed her teeth or done any of her bedtime rituals, but she was such a chicken that she couldn't bear sneaking out of the room to do them now. So she lay there, listening to Rowan's soft breaths, listening for Tanner's footsteps past the door, listening to the beating of her heart until she fell into a restless sleep.

THE WEEKEND CAME and went. Tanner finished painting the railings and then he was home late several nights because of haying. It didn't stop him from doing his odd jobs, though. Sunday, he installed a clothesline, and on Monday, Laura used it for the first time, hanging out Rowan's frilly dresses instead of putting them in the dryer. Then she did the sheets, and loved the smell of them fresh off the line and on the bed.

Another night he unloaded planters from his truck and set them on her step. "Mom had extra bedding plants," he explained. "These ones I can hang as soon as I install some hooks." There were two other large pots with petunias and geraniums. Laura took them and placed them on either side of the door and became ridiculously excited.

"Oh, that's just what we needed around here!"

"She said she's going to do some clippings and if you want some for your yard, to let her know."

"She said that?"

He nodded. "I think she's coming around a little, to be honest."

"I'm glad."

"Me, too. I think it goes a long way for her to know I'm happy."

He was happy. Happy living with *her*. She shouldn't feel so elated about it, but she was. It was a nice feeling, knowing she contributed to someone else's happiness.

"I'm happy, too, Tanner." She smiled. "And it looks so good around here now. With the paint and the flowers and everything."

"Let's show Ro the flowers."

He'd shortened Rowan's name. And he stepped around Laura, went inside and scooped Rowan out of her playpen without any hesitation at all.

Just as a dad would.

No. She wouldn't think like that.

He walked from planter to planter, showing Rowan the brightly colored flowers, letting her gently touch the petals. She heard his deep laugh, and Rowan's higher squeal of excitement. "Do you mind if I take her for a walk around the yard?" he asked. "She seems to like it out here."

"That's fine. Just don't stay out if the bugs are bad. I get the feeling insect bites would be a real pain, you know?"

"Of course."

He gave Rowan a bounce so that she was settled on his arm perfectly, and the two of them set off down the driveway. He'd mowed the lawn, but the ditch had grown and some wildflowers grew there. Laura watched them, Tanner's lips moving as he talked away to Rowan, pointing at things Laura was sure her daughter didn't understand. They stopped at the corner of the property, where a wild rosebush bloomed, the perfume sweet and strong from the pink blossoms. They moved along the edge to the poplar and birch trees, then the circle of spruces. He waved a hand at his face and they turned around to come back.

If she could have handpicked a father for her child, it would be someone like Tanner. Hardworking, honest, caring, fun. Did he even realize how much of a family man he was deep down?

"The bugs were worse toward the backyard. There's a bit of a dip there that holds water."

"It's nearly her bedtime anyway," Laura answered. "I can take her."

When he put Rowan in her arms, their hands brushed. That simple touch was enough to send her stomach into whorls of excitement.

Four more days. Four days from now she'd stand in front of a justice of the peace, his parents and her grandparents to falsely pledge to love and honor him forever. The problem was, it didn't feel so false, and to mean it would only break her heart in the end.

Chapter Thirteen

The phone call came on Thursday, at precisely nine forty-two.

Laura answered it, expecting a final call from the florist in town about the simple bouquet and boutonniere she'd ordered. Instead it was Gavin's partner at the law firm, the lawyer who'd taken on her affairs after Gavin's death.

"Laura, could you come to the office for a meeting this morning?"

Unease rippled through her stomach. "I guess I can get away. Is it important?"

"Nothing to worry about, but I do need to give you an update as soon as possible. My schedule's open this morning. Just tell the receptionist when you get here."

In her experience, *nothing to worry about* was often something to worry about. She hung up the phone feeling slightly sick. The only reason he'd call was if there was news about Spence. The fact that it had happened just three days before her wedding—something she was already nervous enough about—only added to her anxiety.

She didn't often ask her grandmother to watch Rowan, but this morning she did. She had the feeling she needed to be alone at this meeting. She made a quick call, ensuring that Gram was okay to watch Ro for a few hours, and then put together a well-stocked diaper bag, scraped her hair up in a ponytail and swiped a little lip gloss on her lips. That was all she was going to make time for today.

Gram was ready and waiting when she arrived, perked up considerably since her illness and looking like her old self. She took Rowan from Laura's arms and gave her loud kisses in her neck, prompting a belly laugh. "Are you all right, sweetie?" Gram asked. "You sounded upset on the phone."

"It's fine. Just an unexpected appointment that'll be easier without Rowan. I shouldn't be too long. Thanks a million."

"Anytime. We haven't seen her for a while now and she's growing like crazy."

Laura smiled. "I know. Love you, Gram." She kissed her grandmother's cheek. "See you soon."

"Wave bye to your mama," Gram said, lifting Ro's pudgy arm.

Ten minutes later, Laura arrived at the law office; a minute after that the receptionist ushered her into the lawyer's office. To say the quick service made her nervous was an understatement.

"Laura, hello." Richard was middle-aged, with steel-rimmed glasses and salt-and-pepper hair, which gave him an air of both authority and competence. "Have a seat. Can we get you a coffee or anything?"

She swallowed tightly. "With all due respect, you do charge by the hour." She smiled at him, hoping the quip might lighten things for her.

He smiled. "Okay, I know I was kind of cryptic on the phone. You haven't seen the news today, I take it?"

"The news?" She looked at him with some confusion. "No, I don't usually watch in the morning and I hadn't logged on to my computer yet."

"Good. I wanted you to hear it from me, first."

"Hear what?" God, had Spence been paroled? And yet that was hardly something that would make the news. Her blood turned to ice. Escape? Was he coming here? Oh no. She'd left Rowan at Gram's...

Richard reached across the desk. "Forgive me, Laura. I haven't gone about this the right way. You have nothing to fear, all right? Spencer is dead."

The room started to spin. She heard a chair scrape on the floor and a warm, gentle voice beside her. "Okay, now," he said, gently but firmly. "Head between the knees. Try to take deep, slow breaths."

She was hyperventilating. Her heart pounded, her body felt cold and distant, and her head was spinning. She did as she was ordered and dropped her head between her knees, the lawyer's warm hand on her back. It gave her something to focus on until the panic and shock passed and she could breathe again.

"I'm so sorry," she whispered, putting her elbows on her knees and holding her head in her hands. "I wasn't expecting that."

"It's fine. You okay now?"

"Yes, thanks. Though I might like a glass of water."

He disappeared for a moment and then returned with a glass, tinkling with ice cubes. "Here, drink this and I'll fill you in."

The water was cold and refreshing and Laura took a big breath, sitting back in the chair and regaining her composure bit by bit. When Richard was sure of her, he took off his glasses and put them on his desk, then folded his hands and looked at her evenly.

"I'll cut right to the chase, Laura. There was a fight at the prison and Spencer was killed. It's on the news today. I've made a few calls on your behalf, and early reports say he got on the wrong side of someone inside, something gang related. I'm guessing, from what I know of his background and what you and Gavin told me, he probably got a little bit vocal and cocky and someone decided to shut him up."

"He's really dead? Not just injured or something?"

"Really dead. There'll be a full investigation, of course, and I can keep you up to date with that if you like, but mainly my job here today is to tell you that you no longer have to worry about Spencer being a threat. He can't come after you. He can't frighten you anymore, Laura."

She set down the glass, unsure of her feelings. Relief, certainly. This had hung over her head for months, causing so much worry and fear. To know that Spence could never touch her or their child was indeed a relief. But there was sadness, too. Sadness that someone had to die for her to feel safe. She might have wished for a lot of things, and she might even had had the thought that if Spencer were dead, her worries would be over. But she hadn't *truly* wished him dead. She had cared for him once. Sitting in her lawyer's office, she realized that deep down she'd hoped he'd find a way back to being the kind, sweet man she'd first met.

If that man had ever existed.

"It seems so dramatic. Like something out of the movies or cable TV."

"I know." He smiled ruefully. "Laura, Gavin told me what a strong woman you are. I know you've done everything in order to protect your daughter, but don't you think you can let down your guard now? Exonerate yourself—and Gavin?"

"I know." She nodded, a lump forming in her throat. "It wasn't fair to him, or Maddy."

"Or you," Richard added gently. "Now you can set the record straight."

It was too much to process. "First, I need to let this soak in. To see how I feel. To think about what's next."

Next. In three days she was supposed to be marrying Tanner. *Oh my God.* The very reason for their marriage no longer existed. What was she going to do?

She stood and held out her hand. "Richard, I really appreciate you telling me in person. I hope you're not offended when I say I'm glad I won't require your services for a while. At least not in this matter."

He stood, too, and shook her hand. "Not offended at all."

"If your assistant could send me the final bill, that'd be great."

"I'll see to it. Good luck, Laura."

"Thank you, Richard."

She left the office, feeling as if she were walking through a dream.

Outside, the early-summer sun instantly soaked through her light shirt, intense heat in contrast to the air-conditioned comfort of the legal office. She'd gone cold inside, too, so the temperature change was drastic and very welcome. Instead of going to her car, she wandered through town until she arrived at the library. She strolled through the grass, to the bench where she and Tanner had shared doughnuts and coffee, and where she'd decided she could marry him after all.

She couldn't marry him now. And as relieved as she was that Spence could no longer hurt her, she felt incredibly empty when she thought about Tanner not standing beside her at the gazebo on Sunday, or coming in the door at night with a smile, teasing her about her cooking or making faces at Rowan.

She had to tell him. And she needed to do it as soon as possible.

People came and went along the path; the sun moved directly overhead, then passed to her left as time slid by. A dozen possibilities and roadblocks passed through her mind, none of them clear. All she knew—*all she knew*—was that she must be honest with Tanner. She needed to release him from his promise. She'd lied enough over the past year and a half. It was time for truth. Only truth from now on.

Still in a relative daze, she walked back to her car and drove to pick up Rowan. She couldn't leave her at her grandparents' place indefinitely. Laura smiled brightly and told her grandmother everything was absolutely fine, went home and, once Rowan went down for her afternoon nap, called the ranch. Ellen informed her that the boys were out in the fields and wouldn't be back until evening, though she could call out if there was an emergency.

Laura told Ellen it was not an emergency and she'd talk to Tanner in the evening, and then set about trying to keep busy for the rest of the afternoon.

She made dinner, which consisted of pre-breaded chicken breasts, instant rice and frozen vegetables. She certainly didn't trust herself to make anything more involved in her state of mind. She ate alone around seven, tired of waiting and getting hungry since she'd forgotten to eat lunch. She cleaned up the mess, got Rowan ready for bed, saw daylight soften and twilight begin to move in as she tucked her daughter into bed.

The house was cloying, somehow, so she went out on the back landing. Now the space for the chair was shared with a little bucket full of clothespins, as well as a small pot of lavender, the soft scent winding its way around her as she breathed deeply of the night air.

It was nearly dark when she spotted the headlights coming down the road. They disappeared around the front of the house and then swept up the driveway. Tears sprouted in her eyes. She'd only just realized she loved him. Now she had to let him go. Perhaps it was better this way. It would hurt less in the end. Her confusion of this morning had waned and now she saw things clearly. She couldn't go through with the wedding. It wouldn't be fair to either of them.

Laura waited until she heard his voice calling her softly from inside, and then she called back, "Out here."

The patio door slid in its track, strangely loud in the quiet of the night. "What are you doing sitting out here in the dark?" he asked.

"Just thinking. Long day for you, huh?"

"Yeah. Rain forecast for tomorrow, so we wanted to get what we'd cut baled. We worked until we practically couldn't see anymore. Mom said you called the house looking for me."

"I did, yeah. But I didn't want to pull you away when they needed you."

"What's wrong?" He knelt beside her, put his hand on her knee. "You sound down."

"I don't know what I feel. Grab a chair, Tanner. We need to talk."

"That doesn't sound good."

"Actually, it's good news, sort of." She tried to smile. "It's kind of momentous."

He went inside and grabbed a kitchen chair and brought it out on the small landing. She was glad they were outside, where it was dark and he couldn't see her face completely. Her expression was liable to give away her feelings and she needed him to believe her when she told him the truth about Spence.

"Okay," he said, sitting down. "Fire away and tell me what's got you tied up in knots."

"I got a call from my lawyer today."

"This is about Spencer."

"Spence… Yes. He's dead, Tanner. There was some sort of fight and he was stabbed." She'd gone online to read the news and had found out that much. "I don't have to be afraid of him anymore."

Tanner leaned back and blew out a surprised breath. "Wow. You weren't kidding when you said it was big news. It must be wonderful to feel safe again."

Her smile was genuine. "Yes, yes, it does." She sighed. "And sad, too, and a bit guilty. He made his choices, but he could have made different ones. It didn't have to be this way, you know?" She hesitated. "And with him gone, it leaves us with having to make some choices of our own."

There was a beat of silence. "Right. I suppose it does."

"Tanner, the whole reason for us to get married was

so I could change my name, so I could run my business and Spencer couldn't find me when he got out. He's not an issue now, so there's really no reason for us to get married."

"Are you sure?" he asked, the low, silky tone sliding over her.

No, she wasn't damn well sure, but he didn't love her. Like her, yes. She looked at him and her heart swelled.

"Tanner, be serious. You only wanted to get out on your own, and it was a mutually beneficial agreement."

"Right."

"And it's easier to call it off now than if this had happened a week from now. Crazy timing, actually."

Quiet descended. The only sound was the breeze through the leaves on the cottonwoods. Usually, their rustling and tinkling calmed Laura. Tonight, they made her restless.

"You're not saying anything," she noted softly.

He sighed heavily. "I don't know what you want me to say."

"I know the timing is strange, but really, you don't need to feel obligated anymore. Not that you were in the first place. It was incredibly generous of you to help me out of a scrape and I'll never forget it, Tanner. I'll make sure the dresses and everything are returned and you're refunded every penny." She realized she was borderline babbling, but the more she talked, the more nervous she became.

Tanner pushed back his chair with an abrasive scrape and got to his feet. "Shit, do you think I care about the damn dress?" He turned around and rested his elbows on the short railing.

"Then what do you care about, Tanner?"

In the shadows, she saw a muscle tighten in his jaw. "Is it so inconceivable that I might care about you?" he asked, but his voice was grim, not tender.

Had she actually hurt him? She'd only wanted to release him from the arrangement, to convince him that she was okay with it.

"I care about you, too, but this is marriage we're talking about. And if we're not doing it for... What did they used to call them? A marriage of convenience? Then why?" She placed her hand on his shoulder. "Tanner, you married for the wrong reasons before. Do you really want to do that again?"

She saw the hurt on his face, the way his lips turned down, and a rather haunted look appeared in his eyes. "You're not Britt," he said quietly. "You're nothing like her."

"Maybe not," she whispered, "but jumping into marriage would be a mistake, don't you think? We'd set out the rules and reasons before, but now everything's changed. It would be wrong to go ahead with it without...love."

There, she'd said it. Maybe if he said it to her now, she'd be able to tell him how she felt. How the last month together had made her fall in love with him, with the man he was, with the man she could see he wanted to be. How sharing in a laugh and also sharing in his pain had made her feel closer to him than she'd ever felt to another human being.

But instead, he stepped back. "You're right, of course," he murmured. "We started this to give you some anonymity that you don't need anymore. It was a solution to a problem that no longer exists."

It hurt to hear him say it, even though she'd led him to it. "Listen," she said, "I know it's not as cut-and-dried as it might have been. We've…shared things. It's just that marriage is so huge."

"No, I get it. It has to be for the right reasons. Before it was for the greater good. That's all."

She nodded, her heart hurting.

"I can move my stuff out Saturday. I was planning on taking the day before the wedding off anyway."

Alarm shuddered through her. Right. The other benefit to their marriage was him living in her house. She would miss him so much. In just a few weeks, he'd made this place into a home. She looked forward to seeing him at the end of each day. He was someone to talk to and laugh with. Forget her deeper feelings; the basis of their relationship was friendship, and right now that seemed strained at best.

"You don't have to go, Tanner. You could stay. We could be roommates." It wasn't what she wanted from him, but neither would she kick him out. Not when he'd done so much for her.

"I don't think so, Laura. You have the ability to tell the truth about Rowan and Gavin and restore your reputation. You'll never be able to do that if you're living with a guy. No one will believe it's platonic. And Gibson's small, you know that, and old-fashioned. The whole living-together thing, it wouldn't help your situation at all."

"I don't care what people think."

"Yes," he said, "you do."

He didn't say anything more, but then he didn't have to. She did care. The only reason she hadn't spoken up before was because she'd wanted to protect Rowan.

"You have a second chance," Tanner finally said, in a voice that was quiet and sure in the darkness. "You can set the record straight. You can start over. No games, no lies, no fear. A lot of people would give anything to have that. Your decisions can be about what you want for the future, and not about reacting to what's happened in the past. A fresh start, Laura. Reach out and take it."

He was right. He was absolutely right, so why did she feel so awful?

Because she loved him. And because while he proclaimed he cared about her, he didn't love her back.

"You don't need to rush," she responded, trying to keep her voice from shaking. "You can get your things whenever."

"Thanks."

"Where will you go?"

He gave a humorless huff. "Oh, back home at first, I suppose. And then I'll start the apartment search again." He straightened and shoved his hands in his back pockets. "Well, I suppose I'd better get going."

"What?" She blinked in surprise. "You're not going to leave now, are you?"

"Under the circumstances, I think I'll spend the night at the ranch."

"Tanner…"

"Don't sweat it. I have to be there early anyway. This'll cut down on my commute."

Had it really only been days ago he'd said he was happy?

"Don't you want any supper?"

The longer the conversation continued, the firmer his voice became. "I ate at Mom and Dad's."

That was it, then. Somehow there wasn't anything more to say. Nothing to postpone his leaving; no more chances to be honest. It was just *done*.

"I'll be around for my things," he said, squeezing her arm briefly. "I'll let you know when."

All she could do was nod. She found she couldn't speak while her heart was breaking.

He wasn't even all the way out the front door when she began to cry.

Chapter Fourteen

A tap on the window had Tanner stirring from sleep.

Tap. Tap, tap. "Tanner. Get up."

It was Cole. Tanner squinted against the early morning sun and tried to stretch. Oh, right. He'd spent the night in his truck because he'd been too much of a coward to go inside.

"Keep your pants on," he grumbled, knowing Cole probably couldn't hear him. He rubbed his hand over his face and felt the night's growth, rough against his hand. Still groggy, he turned the key in the ignition, just enough to turn on the battery and push the button to lower the window.

"Mornin', sunshine. Trouble in paradise before the wedding?"

He must have looked terrible, because Cole's teasing look fled. "Oh, shit. What happened?"

"I don't wanna talk about it."

"Is there even still a wedding?"

"Cole, please." Dammit, even hours later he could still hear Laura crying. He'd gone out the front door, but she'd been on the back deck and he'd heard it. Faint, but unmistakable.

Stupid thing was, she was the one who'd made

damn sure they didn't go through with this thing. She'd said in no uncertain terms that the reason for their wedding didn't exist anymore.

And then she'd cried about it. He would never, ever understand women.

With a scowl marring his face, Cole went around the front of the truck and got in the passenger side. "You been drinking? You shouldn't be operating machinery if you're hungover."

"God no." Tanner shook his head. "I came here last night, and I just couldn't go inside. I knew you'd ask questions, that Mom would ask, and I just didn't want to talk. So I sat here for a long time. Thinking. And I guess I fell asleep."

Cole smiled a little. "Wouldn't be the first time you slept in your truck."

"Nossir."

They shared a low chuckle, and then Cole said, "What's going on?"

There wasn't much point in hiding the truth now, and besides, Cole already knew bits and pieces. "The guy—Rowan's real father? He was in jail. He was the one killed in the prison fight that was on the news yesterday."

"Holy shit."

"I know. The thing is, Cole, you guys were right in the beginning. This wedding? I was doing it so she could be Laura Hudson. No one would come looking for Laura Hudson, and she could start her own business and be safe. And free."

"Wow. Mighty nice of you, bro."

"Shut up." Tanner knew that knowing tone. Sometimes having a big brother was a pain.

"So the whole thing was for appearances? What was in it for you?"

Tanner sighed. "A place of my own, I guess. And I liked it, too. She's a good roommate. A good friend."

Cole considered for a minute. "More than a friend, Tan?"

"No." The answer came easily enough. "But…"

"Ah," Cole said, leaning back against the seat. "The world-famous 'but.'"

"But she could have been. I really care about her, Cole. And if people knew her the way I know her…and that kid. She's so damn cute. And she likes to cuddle. I wondered before how you could get so attached to Maddy's boys, but it really isn't hard, is it?"

Cole shook his head. "You know what? I think there's more to it than wanting a place of your own. What's going on with you, Tanner? You've been restless for months. I know you like your EMT volunteering, and you're a good rancher, but sometimes it feels like your heart isn't in it."

It wasn't an easy question to answer. It was true. He loved the ranch, but he wasn't as passionate about it as Cole. And he did love his work as a paramedic, even if the town was so small it only warranted a volunteer service. At least he felt that he was helping people. That he was doing something meaningful.

That he had a purpose. He swallowed. There was more to him than a hick cowboy who knew how to two-step and do tequila shots. He'd spent a lot of years enjoying the single life, but once those days were done—right around the time Britt had asked for a divorce—he'd found he didn't have much left.

Tanner glanced at his brother. "If I'm being completely honest, the ranch is your thing. I love it, and I don't mind the work, but it's not really what I want. I want to feel like I'm doing something to help people. To do something important to make someone else's life better. I know that ranching's important, and we provide work and food and preserve the land, but it's not the same."

"Do you want to leave?"

"Tough questions this morning."

"Ones that maybe needed to be asked a while ago." Cole crossed an ankle over his knee and tapped his fingers against his thigh. "Because somewhere in all this, Laura fits in, and you need to figure out where."

Did Tanner want to leave the ranch? Funny thing— the past month or so he'd been far happier at work. He'd caught himself whistling, or humming the tune of a recent song on the radio. There'd been that horrible day when he'd responded to the tractor rollover, but he knew that bad calls were part of the territory. Still, the good had outweighed the bad. And at night he'd gone home to Laura and Rowan.

A lump swelled in his throat. Ever since they'd made their agreement and he'd moved into her house, life had changed. It had become richer, fuller. Maybe being there, with her, was what gave him something to work for.

Her face when she'd seen him fixing the steps, or smiling at him across the table at night had filled him with a simple joy that lifted his heart. Her gentle, understanding touch had helped him get through one of the worst days of his life. She'd tried, too, to do nice things for him. Like when he'd gotten into bed after she hung sheets on the line, and he'd chuckled at the strangely placed puckers where she'd put the clothespins, or how she'd attempted to make doughnuts because she knew they were his favorite.

They'd been far more than roommates. And it had been far more than a legal name change on the line.

Cole's voice was uncharacteristically gentle as he asked, "Do you love her, Tanner?"

Tanner's response was ragged with emotion. "Yes, I think I do."

Cole slapped Tanner's leg. "Well. Hell of a thing, isn't it? Turns a man inside out and scares him to death."

Tanner frowned. "Don't be so smug."

"The way I see it, you have two choices. You can be miserable forever, or you can tell her how you really feel. Maybe she'll send you on your way, but you won't know until you try."

The fact that Laura was crying last night gave him a sliver of hope. "I've had love kick me in the teeth before, you know. I'm not too crazy about taking a chance on a repeat, but if this is the real thing, I think I need to find out."

"Yep. And since the wedding day is almost here, time's a-wastin'. I'm gonna get to work, since it looks like we'll be a man short today. My advice to you is to go inside, let Ma cook you a big breakfast, take a long shower and for God's sake, shave. Then go make your case."

"You always were the bossy one."

"And you, little bro, were the softhearted one who hid behind charm and humor. But I know you. No one can love a woman better than you. You're the kind that goes all in, heart and soul."

"Go on, you're getting all mushy on me. Gross." Tanner shoved Cole's shoulder. "And you're right. I'm hungry and need a shower and a shave."

They both hopped out of the truck, Tanner turning toward the house and Cole to the barns. But then Tanner called back, "Hey, Cole?"

"Yuh."

"Thanks. I needed that."

Cole grinned. "Wasn't that long ago I was in your shoes. Anytime, Tan."

LAURA SLEPT POORLY. Instead of going into Rowan's room, she'd gone to her old room—Tanner's room—and crawled beneath the covers. She didn't want to wake the baby with her crying. But once in there she'd been surrounded by his things, by his scent still in the sheets, and she'd felt a loneliness so profound it was as if someone had bored a hole clear through her, leaving an empty, painful place behind.

Letting him go had been the right thing to do. He didn't need to be obligated to her in any way, nor had he ever been. But oh, she was going to miss him.

In the harsh light of morning, things were no better. Laura took one look at her face and grimaced. She forced herself to take a shower and put on a little makeup so she didn't look as ragged as she felt. Rowan was up and all smiles, which boosted Laura's spirits in some moments and made her sad in others. All she kept thinking was *I love him. And he left.*

But you pushed him away, she reminded herself. *You made sure he wouldn't come back.*

After a good hour and a half of moping, dealing with Rowan's morning routine and using up tissues, she took a deep breath. This was stupid. She'd said that it was only going to be truth from now on, but she hadn't been honest, had she? She'd hidden her true feelings. She'd told him to go and had used their original plan as a shield against being hurt or humiliated. And she'd sent him away, when he was the best thing to happen to her since giving birth to Rowan.

What did she want? She paced the kitchen, stopping to occasionally watch Rowan playing happily in her playpen. She wanted Tanner. She wanted him back in this house. She wanted to kiss him without feeling as if she were breaking a rule, and she wanted to see him holding Rowan in his arms and showing her the flowers and leaves and buzzing insects. He didn't think so, but she knew he'd make a wonderful father. He was patient, kind and loving. She, simply put, wanted Tanner Hudson in her life. For good.

And if that was what she wanted, what was she going to do about it? Tell him the truth? Tell him that she wanted this marriage to go ahead anyway? Tell him that she loved him?

The very idea scared her to death. And yet she knew if she didn't try, she'd regret it forever. The wedding was scheduled for Sunday. She hadn't phoned her grandparents and she had no idea what he'd told his family last night. But she hadn't cancelled the justice of the peace or the flowers or anything. Why?

Maybe because she didn't want to believe it was really over.

For months now, she'd let herself be urged along. All her talk about being strong and independent was a farce. She'd fallen for Spence's charms—that was mistake one. Then she'd accepted Gavin's help, and because of her fear, she'd damaged his reputation along with her own. She had let Tanner come to her rescue... Ugh.

For so long, she'd told herself it was for Rowan's protection, but when it came down to it, she was a coward. And she didn't like herself very much for it. She was better than this. She could be better than this.

If she wanted Tanner back, she needed to make a stand. She would have to conquer the things she'd shied away from. A new hope filled her breast, warm and expansive. She knew the perfect first step. Just as soon as she made a few phone calls.

Chapter Fifteen

Tanner smoothed his already smooth hair and lowered his hand, holding it out in front of him, hoping it was steady. It was not.

Ever since Laura had called the house, asking if they could talk, he'd been a wreck. He was terrified that she wanted to discuss details of canceling everything. Meanwhile, he was trying to work up the nerve to tell her he loved her. And Rowan, too. God, that little girl had him wrapped around her finger.

He looked at the little house that—as recently as yesterday—he'd called home. Plain, but cute. A little paint here, some flowers there. He was proud of the changes he'd made in a few short weeks, knowing they'd made Laura's life a little sunnier. He could do more of that for her. He'd work every day to make it better if that was what he needed to do for them to be together.

Taking a shaky breath, he got out of the truck. He'd put on what he considered dressy clothes—khaki cotton pants and a pale blue button-down shirt, one button open at the neck.

The windows were open, and a delicious smell wafted out of the kitchen. It filled his nostrils as he

climbed the steps. Man, he was as nervous as a teenager on his first date. The smell was vanilla and cinnamon and nutmeg... Oh Lord, had Laura been baking
again? He grinned, loving her even more for her in-
eptitude in the kitchen, not in spite of it. He couldn't
give a good damn if she could cook or not. He'd eat
mac and cheese every day if she'd just say they had a
chance. That she felt the same way about him.

He knocked on the door, slightly sick to his stomach.

The last time he'd shown up with the intent to propose, she'd worn a pretty spring dress. Today she was
wearing jeans and a slate-blue T-shirt, her hair gathered up in a ponytail. With it pulled back from her
face, he noticed how her skin glowed and her eyes
twinkled, big and blue. "Hi," he said, and when she
smiled, it felt as if his tongue thickened and he couldn't
say anything else.

"Come on in, Tanner." She stepped back.

As he entered the kitchen, the first thing he noticed
was the platter of doughnuts.

The kitchen itself was spotless, but a deep fryer sat
on the counter, the only evidence she'd made them herself. Unlike the last burnt offering, these sweets were
perfectly round, with little holes in the middle, and
rolled in plain sugar. They looked—and smelled—
incredible.

"It's a peace offering," she said. "I had some help, of
course. Gram came over and helped so I didn't screw
anything up. Including bringing her deep fryer so I
could regulate the temperature of the grease."

She'd made his favorite thing. Laura, who burned

nearly everything she set her hand to, had made beautiful, golden-brown, delicious-smelling doughnuts.

She picked up the platter and held it out. "Try one," she said, and because she looked so hopeful, he took one, even though eating was the last thing he wanted to do.

The sweet was still warm. The sugar clung to his fingers the moment he picked up the doughnut, and he obligingly took a bite. It was pure heaven. Cakey, not too moist, not dry, rich with cinnamon and nutmeg. He chewed and swallowed, then smiled at her. "Delicious. So good."

Her face relaxed, pleased with his verdict. "God, I'm so relieved," she said, putting the plate down on the table.

"You didn't try one?" He took another bite. Half-wished for a glass of cold milk to wash it down with, but he wasn't going to ask.

She shook her head, her ponytail bobbing. "I couldn't eat," she admitted. "I was too nervous."

He finished the doughnut and brushed the sugar off his hands. "Nervous? About what?"

She bit her lip. "About seeing you. About the things I need to say that I didn't say last night."

"Me, too," he admitted.

The color drained from her face. "Can I go first, Tanner? I think I really need to get this off my chest."

Maybe he wouldn't have to tell her at all. A peace offering might only mean she wanted to preserve their friendship, when what he wanted was so much more. If she shut him down, what point would there be in telling her how he felt?

"Do I need to sit down for this?"

She shook her head. "Rowan's asleep. Let's take a walk outside for a few minutes. It's about time I enjoyed my yard, I think."

She slid on a pair of sandals and they headed outside, walking across the grass towards the trees where it was cooler. The early-afternoon sun was hot and welcome, and Tanner briefly thought of his brother and father out haying today. He felt a little guilty, not being with them, but also as though this day was an important one for his future.

They stopped by the rosebush. Laura tentatively reached out, being careful of thorns, and plucked a delicate pink blossom from the shrub.

"I love wild roses, don't you?" she asked. "They're so soft and pretty and smell so nice, and yet they're hardy and grow just about anywhere. Even in this yard, where the ground is hard and the drainage isn't great, here they are."

Tanner peered down at her, more sure than ever that he was in love with her. "Is this some sort of metaphor, Laura?"

She looked up at him, squinting a little against the sunlight. "Yes, it is. I'd like to think that I've become stronger the last few months."

"You've always been strong," Tanner began, but Laura shook her head and cut him off.

"No, I haven't. I've hidden behind my situation. I've used my fear as a crutch. I've hurt people telling myself it was for the greater good. But it was selfish of me, Tanner. Last night, I lied to you. I had promised myself after I saw the lawyer that I would only tell the truth from now on. And then, only hours later when you were in front of me, I lied." She turned the flower around and around in her fingers. "I need to tell you the truth now."

"Which is?"

The flower stopped spinning. "I love you, Tanner. I know that wasn't the plan. I know I wasn't supposed to. But I do anyway. I love your kindness, and your sense of humor, your duty, and honor. I love your big heart and the way you make me feel like I'm somebody. I love the way you hold my daughter in your arms, and the way you look at her when you think I'm not looking. This was supposed to be a mutually beneficial arrangement, but I broke the rules. I fell in love with you."

The rose trembled in her hand. "I don't expect you to feel the same way. And Lord knows it's fast and I come with a crap ton of baggage. But I promised to tell the truth and that's it. I love you."

It was so unexpected, so heartfelt and…for God's sake, she'd given him an itemized list of what she liked about him. It was almost too much to comprehend. But the one phrase that stuck in his brain, keeping it all together, was "I love you."

He took the nearly wilted flower from her nervous fingers and tucked it gently behind her ear. "I slept in my truck last night," he confessed, unsure of where to begin, but knowing he'd somehow get to the right point eventually. "I couldn't stand the idea of going inside and answering questions. I was so confused, you see. Taking Spencer out of the equation changed everything, and made me look long and hard at us and what we might look like without him pushing us together."

He brushed his thumb over the crest of her cheek.

"It forced me to look at why I was marrying you. And I figured out it wasn't so I could have a place of my own, or even so you could change your name. Those were just excuses. The reasons I told myself. But deep down it was something more. It was me searching for meaning in my life."

She pulled his hand down from her face. "Tanner, I know you're not a hundred percent happy on the ranch. I know you volunteer as a paramedic because you like helping people. But I can't be some pet project to make you feel better. Not now. Last night, I said that marriage had to be for the right reasons, and I still believe that."

"No, no, you don't understand." Instead of letting her drop his hand, he linked his fingers with hers, holding them tightly. "What I mean is, my thinking that there had to be something more was true, but it doesn't have to do with the ranch or a job or anything like that. The something more I needed was for in here." He lifted their joined hands and pressed them to his heart. "When everything went wrong a few years ago, I told myself I was not the marrying kind. After all, that's what I'd been told. That I was good for a good time, but not forever. But she was wrong, Laura. *She* was built that way, not me. I believed what she said for far too long until you showed me something different. Turns out, I'm not a party guy. I'm a family man. The weeks spent here, with you…that's the happiest I ever remember being. Fixing the little things around here was a joy because it felt, well, it felt like I was doing it to my home, too. The thing is, Laura, we've been playing house. And I don't want to play. I want it to be real."

"By real, you mean?"

"I mean," he said, his heart clubbing against his ribs, "that I fell in love with you, too. With your sweetness, and the way you love your daughter, and the compassion you have deep inside. That day when I came home and you'd burned those silly doughnuts…" He squeezed her fingers, gazed into her eyes. "That was such a horrible day. But you sat with me, and held me, and made everything better. You cared for me in a way no one has ever done before. You treated me…" His voice broke a little. "Honey, you treated me like the man I wanted to become, rather than the man I thought I was."

Tears gathered in her eyes. "You really love me?"

He nodded. "I do. And you are stronger than you think, you know. I knew that the day I sat in the back of the ambulance and held your hand as you brought Rowan into the world. You were fierce, and gorgeous, and beautiful. I think both our lives changed that day. You became a mom, and I caught a glimpse of what my life was meant to be." He drew her close and looped his arms low around her back. "With you. If you'll still have me."

She didn't answer. But she didn't have to, either, because she jumped up on tiptoe and wrapped her arms around his neck, hugging him close. He closed his eyes and tightened his embrace, feeling all the pieces of his life that had been flung far and wide last night click back into place.

They held each other for a few minutes, enjoying the sensation of giving their feelings liberty at last. When Laura pulled back, Tanner kept one hand on the curve of her back and put the other beneath her chin, cupping it gently in his fingers. Then he finally kissed her the way he'd wanted to for weeks. With nothing between them—no arrangement, no worry about what was appropriate, no secrets. Just love, and the simmering attraction they'd been denying for too long.

"Mmm," she murmured against his lips. "It feels good to finally do that."

"I know," he said, kissing the tip of her ear. "Know what's better? We can do that anytime we want now."

"But I might not get anything done, because I'll want to do it all the time."

He chuckled, down low. "It?" When she blushed, he wanted to wrap her in his arms and hold her close forever. "Sweetheart, this might seem stupid and traditional of me, but I kind of like the idea of waiting for the wedding night."

Blushing or not, she lifted her chin defiantly. "Well, I can wait a little longer if you can."

"You still want to go through with the wedding?"

She nodded. "I'm sure, Tanner. We have the place, and the justice of the peace, and I have the dress. It feels right. I want you here with me, and with Rowan." She touched his face. "I want you to be her daddy, and show her flowers, and teach her to ride a horse and read her stories at bedtime."

He was so honored, so humbled. Every decision Laura had made in the last year and a half had been for Rowan. For her to choose him, to trust him... "I want that, too," he said. "And someday, maybe a few more."

She grinned. "Holy cats. We're going to do this, aren't we?"

He nodded, then lifted her up by the waist and held

her tightly. "Yes, we are. And we're going to do it for the right reasons."

"For love," she said.

"For love."

Chapter Sixteen

Every bride wanted a sunny day for her wedding, and at dawn Laura wasn't sure that was what she'd get. But then around 9:00 a.m., the showers stopped, the clouds drifted away and the sky turned a brilliant blue with a few white puffs gliding along for contrast.

She was getting married today. Today!

The ceremony was at two, with a small tea and sweets reception to follow at her grandparents' house. They'd insisted on hosting, as Laura's only family present, and she'd been touched. Now the day would be even more special because she and Tanner didn't have to pretend to be in love. They were truly in love, and it was marvelous.

After she'd fed Rowan lunch, Laura put her down for an early nap. Then she went to work dressing, putting on her makeup and twisting her hair into a low, classy chignon at the base of her skull. She teased loose a few pieces of hair at the side of her face to give herself more of a romantic look. Inspired, she put on some old shoes and walked through the wet grass to the rosebush. She clipped a couple of blossoms and put the stems in a damp paper towel.

Once Rowan woke, Laura changed her and put her

in the pink ruffled dress she and Tanner had bought, and slipped tiny white shoes on her feet. With excitement drumming through her veins, Laura tucked the ring she'd bought for Tanner into her purse, made sure the diaper bag was stocked and rushed out the door to make the last stop before the park: the florist.

By the time she got to the parking area near the gazebo, she saw her grandparents' car and Tanner's truck already there. Cole and Maddy had arrived, too. Cole was dressed in a suit, but with the customary black boots and hat. She smiled, and then she saw Tanner. He was dressed exactly the same as Cole, and her heart thumped in approval. No matter what he said, he was her cowboy. Everyone was milling about together when Tanner finally noticed their arrival. 3Laura's new pumps made clicking sounds on the asphalt of the parking lot.

He came forward, all long strides and big smiles. "Hello, bride."

"Hello, groom." She had Rowan on one arm and her bouquet in her other hand. Without missing a beat, Tanner reached for Rowan and Rowan put out her arms for him.

"Hello, sweetheart," he said, dropping a kiss on her head. "You look so pretty."

He looked down at Laura. "After today, I get to be her daddy."

"Yes, you do," she said. "Isn't she lucky?"

Tanner planted a firm kiss on Laura's lips.

"Hey, now, you two. None of that until the end of the ceremony. Sheesh. Don't you know anything?"

Cole was teasing. Maddy smiled beside him, and

even Tanner's parents looked happier about the wedding than they had the last time Laura saw them.

And Gramps—well, he was grinning from ear to ear and held Gram's hand as if they were twenty again.

They all walked to the gazebo, where the justice of the peace waited. Just before they got there though, Laura paused. "Maybe Gram could hold Rowan during the ceremony? Besides, you're missing something."

As Tanner handed off the baby, Laura plucked the wild rose from her bouquet. She'd had the florist bind the stem and substitute it for the white rose boutonniere she'd ordered. The other rose was tucked into Laura's hair. "Let me pin this on you," she said, smiling up at him.

The pink was a few shades darker than her dress, but it didn't matter. They both knew the flowers had meaning, and Tanner held her simple bouquet of roses and alstromeria while she pinned the blossom on his lapel.

"Now I think we're ready." She put her hand briefly on his chest.

"I know I'm ready," he said.

He took her hand and they climbed the gazebo steps together. Made promises, gave each other rings, sealed it with a kiss. It was remarkably short, but Laura committed every moment to her memory. She couldn't take her eyes off Tanner, and sniffled when he whispered, "I love you" after he kissed her.

But the best part was when they were announced as Tanner and Laura Hudson. That, she decided, felt like victory.

SHE DIDN'T GET a chance to speak to Maddy until they were drinking champagne at her grandparents' place.

The bubbly had been a surprise, and meant all the more because it came from Tanner's mom and dad. Laura knew more than one truth needed to be set right, so she found Maddy and offered her a piece of wedding cake.

Laura put down the plate and touched the woman's arm. "Maddy, there's something I need to say to you."

"Sure." Her response was much more relaxed than it had been in the past. Laura wondered if one day they might be friends, as well as sisters-in-law. It went without saying that Cole would pop the question one of these days.

"Letting people think Gavin was the father of my baby was wrong. I don't know why I ever thought it was a good idea, other than I was scared. But I could have found another way. I made you promise not to say anything before, but I release you from that now. If you want to set the record straight about Gavin at any point, you're free to do so. And I'll do the same."

"Thank you, Laura. Though it really doesn't matter now, does it?"

Laura shrugged. "Someday Rowan will be going to school with your boys. They don't need to deal with that kind of thing. I'm not planning on taking a page out in the paper or anything, but I'll do what I can to restore his reputation. He was too good a man."

Maddy smiled wistfully. "Yes, he was. And now we've both ended up with good men."

Laura laughed and glanced over at Tanner, talking with his brother. "I don't know what I did to deserve Tanner, but I'm feeling pretty blessed."

"You truly do love him."

"I didn't plan to. Tried not to." She winked at Maddy. "I hear you know what that's like."

They laughed a little, but then Laura sobered. "Thank you, Maddy. For being here today. For being so forgiving."

Maddy smiled. "I got that from Cole. And I'm glad to see Tanner happy. The rest we'll figure out as we go along."

Cole looked over and touched his watch. Maddy sighed. "I'm sorry. I've left the boys at my mom's, but they have plans tonight. We have to dash out."

"Of course. I'm just glad you and Cole came. It meant a lot to both of us."

To her surprise, Maddy gave her a quick hug. "Congratulations."

When Maddy had darted away, Tanner came over. "Mrs. Hudson, did Maddy just hug you?"

She smiled. "Yes, she did. And please, call me Mrs. Hudson some more. I like it."

"Mrs. Hudson." His smile was lopsided and he dropped a kiss on her lips. Then he slid behind her and put his arms around her, so her back was pressed against his chest. She felt safe and secure in his arms. She looked around the room. The people they cared about most were here. Cole and Maddy were just making their way out to pick up the twins. Laura's grandmother and grandfather were ensconced on the sofa, still holding hands. Tanner's mom, Ellen, held a very sleepy Rowan in her arms, while John sat in an armchair and talked to Charlie about the ongoing issue of installing a traffic light in town.

"Happy?" he asked.

Laura put her hands over his forearms and held him close. "The happiest," she said.

And she was.

* * * * *

REQUEST YOUR FREE BOOKS!
2 FREE NOVELS PLUS 2 FREE GIFTS!

HARLEQUIN®

American Romance®

LOVE, HOME & HAPPINESS

HAR15

*Josh Dempsey has always seemed
reserved and distant to Cara Alvarez. But maybe
he's not the man she thinks he is...*

Read on for a sneak peek of
COME HOME, COWBOY by New York Times
bestselling author *Cathy McDavid.*

A soft, concerned and decidedly male voice interrupted her from just outside the corral.

"Are you all right?"

She quickly gathered herself, using the sleeve of her denim jacket to wipe her face. "I'm fine," she said, sounding stronger than she felt.

"You sure?"

She dared a peek over the top of Hurry Up's mane, only to quickly duck down.

Josh Dempsey, August's oldest son, stood watching her. She recognized his brown Resistol cowboy hat and tan canvas duster through the sucker rod railing. Of all the people to find her, why him?

Heat raced up her neck and engulfed her face. Not from embarrassment, but anger. It wasn't that she didn't like Josh. Okay, to be honest, she didn't like him. He'd made it clear from the moment he'd arrived at Dos Estrellas a few months ago that he wanted the land belonging to the mustang sanctuary.

She understood. To a degree. The cattle operation was the sole source of income for the ranch, and the sanctuary—operating mostly on donations—occupied a significant amount of valuable pastureland. In addition,

Cara didn't technically own the land. She'd simply been granted use of the two sections and the right to reside in the ranch house for as long as she wanted or for as long as the ranch remained in the family.

Sympathy for the struggling cattle operation didn't change her feelings. She needed the sanctuary. She and the two-hundred-plus horses that would otherwise be homeless. For those reasons, she refused to concede, causing friction in the family.

Additional friction. Gabe Dempsey and his half brothers, Josh and Cole, were frequently at odds over the ranch, the terms of their late father's will and the mustang sanctuary.

"You need some help?" Josh asked from the other side of the corral.

"No."

"Okay."

But he didn't leave.

Without having to glance up, she felt his height and the breadth of his wide shoulders. He looked at her with those piercing blue eyes of his.

She'd seen his eyes flash with anger—at his brother Gabe and at her for having the audacity to stand up to him. She'd also seen them soften when he talked about his two children.

"I'm sorry," he said with a tenderness in his voice that she'd never heard before. "Violet told me earlier. About your son."

*Don't miss COME HOME, COWBOY by Cathy McDavid, part of the **MUSTANG VALLEY** miniseries, available February 2016 wherever Harlequin® American Romance® books and ebooks are sold.*

HARLEQUIN®

A *Romance* FOR EVERY MOOD™

JUST CAN'T GET ENOUGH?

Join our social communities
and talk to us online.

You will have access to the latest
news on upcoming titles and special
promotions, but most importantly,
you can talk to other fans about your
favorite Harlequin reads.

Harlequin.com/Community

Facebook.com/HarlequinBooks

Twitter.com/HarlequinBooks

Pinterest.com/HarlequinBooks

THE WORLD IS BETTER WITH

Romance

Harlequin has everything from contemporary, passionate and heartwarming to suspenseful and inspirational stories.

Whatever your mood, we have a romance just for you!